A SOLITARY DANCE

SERRELL & SIMONS *Wisconsin*

A SOLITARY DANCE

A NOVEL
BY
ROBERT LANE

THIS IS A LOTUS BOOK
PUBLISHED BY SERRELL & SIMONS

Serrell & Simons, Publishers
Box 64
Winnebago, Wisconsin 54985

Library of Congress Cataloging in Publication Data
Lane, Robert G.
A solitary dance
I. Title   82-81020
ISBN Hardbound 0-943104-82-3 $11.95
ISBN Softbound 0-943104-83-1 $6.95

Acknowledgment is hereby made for permission
from Alfred A. Knopf to quote from
The Prophet, 1923, 1957, by
Kahlil Gibran.

Book design by Mary Lane
Printed in the United States of America
1983

ACKNOWLEDGMENTS

MY DEEPEST APPRECIATION TO MY BEST FRIEND MARY, who has been nothing short of superb throughout this endeavor; to Ted Solotaroff, a gently supportive editor who lent his considerable skills as this story took shape; and to my six-year-old niece Shelby, who was kind enough to help me with the illustrations.

I am grateful to them, and to the many others who contributed along the way.

A NOTE ABOUT THIS STORY

THERE ARE THOUSANDS OF CHILDREN SUCH AS I HAVE described here. Living in group homes, treatment centers, mental hospitals across the land, they are called by many names—schizophrenic, emotionally disturbed, autistic. Yet beneath the symptoms that contribute to such diagnoses, one often finds a common denominator: an exquisitely sensitive, confused, lonely youngster. A child who longs not only to be loved, but to be able to love in return.

This story is for each of those special children, and for the people who care for them. It was written with the hope that it will help others have a better understanding of the emotional disorders of childhood.

What I have tried to do is to capture the essence of my experiences, both as a psychotherapist and as a supervising therapist and teacher. Because of that, the story rings true. All of what I have written here, though, is fictitious— the end product of a very active imagination. Hence, any resemblances to real individuals, situations, or institutions are pure and simple coincidence, and nothing more.

A SOLITARY DANCE

*And in the sweetness of friendship let there
be laughter, and sharing of pleasures.
For in the dew of little things the heart finds
its morning and is refreshed.*

KAHLIL GIBRAN

CHAPTER ONE

DESTINIES HAVE A WAY OF INTERTWINING, SOMETIMES taking extraordinary turns when least expected. On Michael Harris's fifth birthday, he was committed to the children's unit of a psychiatric hospital. He was still there three years later when I arrived as an intern in clinical psychology. That's how our paths crossed.

Merrick State Hospital is probably the most picturesque of any of the institutions run by California's Division of Mental Hygiene. It lies in a remote mountainous area north of Santa Barbara, straddling a line between the dark fertile hills and valleys of citrus groves that flow down to the coast and the rugged mountains that rise up to the east. There the terrain is desolate enough that only the wiry manzanita brush can survive.

The entrance to the hospital grounds is through two stone pillars set imposingly on each side of the macadam road that curves innocuously back among the hills. Except for the brass plaques inscribed Merrick State Psychiatric Hospital, there is no evidence of an institution.

My first reaction to Merrick was that the site had been chosen by people who regarded mental disorders as something to be hidden from public view. Unless you worked there, or were a patient or visitor, you would hardly suspect that tucked into such pretty countryside were hundreds of mental patients, all of them sufficiently disturbed to be committed and some of them so dangerous that they were kept in a maximum security wing.

The buildings that finally came into sight had high walls of dull yellow brick and red-tiled roofs that created a dramatic contrast to the rolling lawns and blue sky. Yet despite the very tasteful architecture, the manicured grounds and abundant shade trees, the picnic tables and other amenities, the impression lingered that I had entered a modern-day leper colony whose principal function was to quarantine undesirables. Everything appeared to go on indoors. Though the parking lots were filled with cars, there was hardly anyone to be seen. At each intersection white signs with neat black lettering indicated the numbered dormitories, the food service building, a general hospital. It was like a medium-sized college campus. Except that the lack of any visible activity, the silence, were eerie.

At the last intersection, the road left the main hospital grounds and followed a series of bends that led into an offshoot canyon and the Children's Unit. This was made up of a circle of a half-dozen cottages, plain and functional. There were noticeably more signs of life here—a few youngsters darting about, then a football arching up, only to land on a cottage roof, accompanied by shouts of dismay. On the far side of the quad, beneath the branches of a live oak, a group was gathered around a teacher. From a

distance it could have been an ordinary class in any elementary school. Nearby was a small school building, its
playground surrounded by a cyclone fence sagging with
fatigue. Everything seemed quite commonplace.

The name on the open door matched the one written
on the moist paper I was tightly grasping. Not wishing to
startle the man who was intently studying a large packet of
papers, I knocked lightly on the doorframe. Dr. Scott, the
chief psychologist of the Children's Unit, glanced up, his
eyes crinkling with a welcoming smile.

"Patrick McGarry, is it?" I nodded and reached for the
extended hand. "Call me Scott," he said. "It serves nicely as
both my first and last names."

Right away I liked him—a trim man in his middle
years with short gray hair brushed haphazardly to one
side. He was low-key and informal, his feet resting in a
small clearing of an otherwise overflowing desk.

"And how is Warfield, the old warhorse?"

"Fine, he sends his regards." Dr. Warfield, my advisor
at Cal State, had arranged for me to spend my yearlong
internship on the Children's Unit. He and Scott were old
friends; I had heard many stories about their escapades.

After talking for a time, Scott suggested taking a walk
around the unit so that I could get my bearings. The warm
and direct manner was soon put to the test by a crowd of
children who trailed after him as we strolled about the
grounds.

"Hi, Dr. Scott—lookit me, lookit me!"

"Hey, Dr. Scott, got any gum?"

"Dr. Scott, Dr. Scott, can I go home this weekend?
Pleeeeeze? It's my friend's birthday and I'm invited to his

party, and I've done all my assignments, and my folks say it's okay with them, and everyone says I've been good all week, and . . . "

He was steadily besieged by youngsters requesting favors, hanging onto him, tugging at his coat, grabbing his hands. With each one he stopped, talked, joked around, once tousling a curly mop to see who was under it and suggesting sheepshears. He listened attentively and patiently to each child and gave firm, unevasive answers—not always the ones the kids wanted to hear, but they seemed to accept even the negative ones. As I watched, my respect for him grew rapidly.

After the first wave of children had been dispatched, Scott motioned to one of the larger cottages and we started across the lawn toward it.

"You know," I said, "I can't help being surprised. For kids who are supposed to be so deeply disturbed that they need hospitalization . . . well, they're not at all what I expected. They don't seem that much different from ordinary kids."

Scott nodded. "They're not . . . generally. But just now you've seen the ones who relate fairly well, the ones who've figured out who signs the home passes and grants other privileges. And they can be pretty good kids if there's something in it for them. But don't let your guard down for a minute. Or be inconsistent with them. That'll set them off every time."

By then we had reached the entrance and Scott turned. "This is the autistic children's ward. Let's go in for a few minutes—I want you to see some of our more difficult cases. Probably more like what you expected."

He flipped through a huge key ring, opened the door, and motioned me in.

Instant, unbelievable chaos.

Scattered about a large tiled room were some twenty-five children, each in his or her own singular frenzy, but collectively creating a state of pandemonium. Some were spinning like tops, careening recklessly around the room. Others sat on the floor rocking back and forth in awkward, jerky kinds of motions, while others jumped or ran, hurling themselves across the room like unguided missiles. Still others crouched alone in different corners, babbling to themselves or waving splayed fingers before their faces.

A few of the children wore padded mittens and football helmets. They looked odd at first, until one little girl suddenly hit herself on the side of the head five or six times and shrieked, "No, no, NO, NOOOO!!!"

Then she ceased as abruptly as she had begun.

Scott touched me on the shoulder and as I turned, a youngster sprinted by me, running full tilt.

"Got to watch yourself here," Scott said.

Then another small boy, no more than five, walked up to me and wrapped his arms around my leg. As I bent down to talk to him, another came and put his arm on my shoulder, trying to burrow his face into my hair.

I tried to talk to the two children, but there was no intelligible response. I recalled reading somewhere that a conversation with an autistic child is like talking to the walls. It's worse. And more unnerving. They just stared right through me. Finally I had to untangle the encircling octopus arms of my new friends. They resisted at first but then moved away, each returning to his own isolated activity.

"These are the really tough ones," Scott said as we left. "The ones we can't seem to reach. You'll be putting in a bit of time here."

Doing what, I wondered. I just couldn't comprehend how young, physically healthy children could act in such grotesque ways. Of course, I had read about infantile autism, but nothing had prepared me for the reality of the actual children—kids who battered themselves, or chewed their lips bloody, or sat immobilized in stiff, awkward postures.

What had life become for them? And what, if anything, could anyone do for them? The realization began to seep in that I would be expected to come up with something. And then a sinking feeling came in an icy wave: It seemed like such a hopeless task. What if I couldn't hack it?

Scott seemed to sense my misgivings and we walked along in silence while I tried to sort through the jumble of images and reactions. For years now I thought I had known what I was going to be getting into. But in my practica experiences at the university clinic, the children had all been capable of interacting on some level at least, and none had been so severely disturbed.

Just as I had begun to regain my composure, Scott slowed, then pointed toward a slight figure standing behind a bush near an adjacent cottage. "Let's go over there, Pat. I want to show you a rather classic example of childhood schizophrenia."

He approached the boy, who was propped rigidly against the brick wall, staring down at the ground.

"Hi, Danny, how're you doing?"

Danny, who looked to be eight or nine years old, slowly raised his head. His dark wavy hair was parted perfectly, each hair fastidiously in place. But it was his deep-set eyes that captured my attention; they were a soft moss green, and incredibly remote. Glazed, too, perhaps by an antipsychotic drug. Thorazine, or Mellaril? His eyes turned toward us in a blank stare. Then his arm moved ponderously, almost in slow motion like a robot's, as he withdrew a dirty sheaf of papers from his pocket. In a steady monotone that reminded me of a rocketry engineer's discussion of critical orbital calculations, Danny began to tell us about the mathematical computations that covered some twenty smudged pages. His child's voice seemed strangely incongruous.

"This is the X factor; if you multiply four billion, 300 million, 500 thousand by three hundred and sixty-five you get this figure, and if then for each day you subtract this constant of six million, it will give you the latitude and longitude you need for the computation of the Y factor . . ."

Danny droned on, using familiar words and concepts, but stringing them together in a litany of uncontrolled imagination. Meanwhile he leafed through the pages, some of which were refolded so many times they had the look of parchment. Scott listened for a time, as patiently as if it were their first encounter. None of what Danny was saying made sense but, following Scott's lead, I nodded my head occasionally while glancing at the intense little boy running his ink-stained, pudgy finger across the pages of numbers. I tried to decode the reasoning behind his calculations, but it seemed totally simulated. Such a conspicuously bright youngster—what could have happened to him?

"That looks fine, Danny," Scott finally broke in. "But come on, let's go spend some time with the other children, too, okay?"

He put his arm around the youngster's shoulders. Danny put up no resistance, allowing himself to be guided from the bushes to a group of children sitting on the lawn not far away. Silently he took his place in the circle without seeming to be aware of the others.

As we moved away, Scott said, "Danny came here just six months ago. As you can see, he's very delusional. I wish we could've gotten him sooner—we might've been able to do more for him. . . ."

I looked back at Danny, who had folded his grimy little papers along their familiar creases and was stuffing them back into his pocket. I was suddenly struck by the terrible isolation he must feel; the calculations seemed to be his only conduit to people—and yet no one could understand them.

Scott broke into my thoughts.

"Cottage 4 over there is where we house the younger schizophrenic kids, like Danny."

I glanced at the long low building. It looked like all the others. At the far end, though, the large metal door stood propped open. Scott stopped, rubbing his chin thoughtfully.

"That's odd, the—"

Suddenly, a small hunched figure dashed from the cottage and disappeared behind a low wall.

"What on earth was that?"

"Ah, yes, that explains it," Scott nodded, his gaze sweeping along the wall. "That," and he sighed, "is Merrick's very own feral child. Mike?" he called out.

The top of a head peeked over the wall.

"Hi, Mike—I thought that was you. How are you?"

The head vanished.

I tried to focus on this new shock. "A feral child?"

"Well, it's not much of an exaggeration. He's eight years old, been here for three years, and goes into a frenzy if an adult comes within twenty-five feet of him. Watch him eat sometime. He just wolfs down his food, grunting and making weird sounds—like a wild animal. And I guess every chance he gets, Mike roams the hills back there. We've given up trying to contain him—he can always find a way out." Scott nodded toward the high boundary fence that encircled the compound. Behind it brush-covered hills thrust steeply upward, saw-toothed and scarred by countless rock slides. It looked like formidable terrain.

Just then, out of the corner of my eye I saw another fleeting movement. A head of wildly chopped blond hair appeared, and a pair of intent glistening eyes, alert as a lynx's, were inspecting us again.

I waved.

Once again, the head vanished.

"We're being observed and followed," said Scott. "That's why we call him the Little Shadow. But he never comes any closer. That's what's so frustrating. He'll follow at a distance—you can sense he wants to make contact— yet the minute you try to approach him, he's off like a shot."

I scanned the length of the wall while we stood there a few minutes longer, but the child didn't reappear. Something about his eyes seemed vaguely familiar to me, though. A "feral child"—it seemed fantastic in this century. By the time we reached the administration building, Scott had told me everything he knew about Mike.

The next day Scott showed me some diagnostic test reports and outlined my responsibilities. "We'll be rotating you around to the various cottages so you'll have some contact with nearly all of the youngsters and will be able to get a feel for the kinds of treatment programs we have here.

There'll be diagnostic reports and progress notes and all the bureaucratic paperwork that the state requires. And later on you'll be doing some admission interviews. For now, though, I want you to give some thought to working with one of the children."

I knew this would be coming eventually, but Scott had caught me by surprise. After what I had seen yesterday, I wasn't at all sure I was ready for it. Suppose I were assigned to one of those autistic kids in the football helmets?

As though reading my mind, Scott said, "You seemed quite interested in Mike, our Little Shadow. Do you think you might like to try working with him? Or would you rather wait a bit until you get to meet some of the other youngsters?"

"I don't know . . ." I began.

But then, I did know. There had been something very intriguing about that goofy little kid scooting around, stalking us, furtively poking his head out at intervals. I'd found myself thinking about him on the drive home last night, wondering what had happened to him, how one might begin to reach him. He had dimly reminded me of some other people I'd known and felt close to—a solitary beach rat named Charlie I'd philosophized with during my surfing years, and Lars, a deeply reclusive odd-jobs man I'd become friendly with during the winters when I was a ski bum. Both of them had had a special air of desolation, a quality that I recognized even then as an extension of my own solitariness. I sensed something similar in Mike, although his was certainly a far more extreme version.

"You know, I guess I might like to have a go at him. What do you think?"

"Well, he'll be a tough one. For one thing, Mike's been here for quite a few years now and, as I told you, no one has been able to make a dent so far. It'll take a lot of work and patience—and you may not get much in the way of results. It often takes a long time to get anything going with these kids, but with Mike . . . "

"That's okay," I said as confidently as I could. "That's why I'm here."

Scott smiled noncommittally. "I had a hunch you'd want to take him on." He handed me a heavy folder, jammed with institutional records, case history, progress notes, school reports.

Later, back in my office, I sat and stared at the enormous file. It represented a person, a child—eight fragile years of life distilled into a three-inch-thick mass of papers. I felt vaguely repelled, not really wanting to scrutinize it, to be guided by the reams of words that had been dictated, typed in triplicate, initialed, and dutifully filed. The whole process seemed too impersonal and futile. Finally, however, my curiosity got the better of me and I began to thumb through the pages.

CHAPTER TWO

ADMISSION NOTE

Name: Michael Harris
Age: 5 years, 0 months
Diagnosis: Schizophrenia; Childhood Reaction
Psychiatric Impairment: Maximal
Prognosis: Poor

This five-year-old child is quite psychotic, autistic, and hyperactive; he is ritualistic and regressed in both speech and movement, seemingly paying no attention to people in his environment; speech behavior ranging from muteness to jabbering in a singsong voice that is marked by a severe speech impediment; thinking disorganized and judgment, insight, and reasoning very defective; he is intensely fascinated with running water, fires.

Parents report child is unable to attend school, unable to get along with other children or people, and needs constant supervision because of starting fires, wrecking things, and stuffing paper up his nose.

According to the case history, Mike was the only child of a woman who had been hospitalized several times for what was described only as a "nervous breakdown." Mrs. Harris was twenty-eight when Mike came to Merrick and was said to be unkempt and "thin as a rail," a highly emotional and unstable person with so little confidence in herself that she was almost totally reliant upon her husband. Tom Gazarro, the psychiatric social worker who did the intake interview, felt she was a borderline psychotic. It was difficult for him to get an accurate history, but it seemed that shortly after Mike was born, Mrs. Harris had become very depressed and began to believe that her son was exposing her to an onslaught of "germs." She handled him as little as possible, convinced that Mike would make her sick if she spent too much time with him or got too close to him. Contact was limited to giving him a bottle or changing his diapers.

Responsibility for Mike had rested mainly with the father; he was described as a rather slight, volatile man— "a bantam rooster"—whose conversation was laced with quotes from the Bible. He ignored his wife's bizarre ideas and behavior, acting as if she were as sane as the next person. An assembly line worker, Mr. Harris had boasted of his recent election as a shop steward, but he acknowledged that his long working hours prevented him from spending much time with his son.

The parents could not remember clearly at what age Mike had sat up, crawled, walked, talked, been toilet trained. About all they could contribute was that he was a "fussy baby," sick a lot, and that his strange behavior began when he was about three. Evidently that had been when Mike moved toward schizophrenia, filling the vacuum in his life with fantasy figures, routines, and communications until, at the age of four, his teeming imagination and profoundly frustrated feelings began to overwhelm him.

And then I hit the shocker. The pediatrician who had referred the family was convinced that Mike was trying to commit suicide. . . .

I leaned back in my chair and thought about *that* one. How is it even *possible* for a child that young to comprehend committing suicide? But, according to the parents, about eight months prior to his admission, Mike had begun to hold his breath and, shortly thereafter, to stuff paper, cloth—whatever was handy—into his nose and mouth. He would gag and roll around on the floor in apparent attempts to stop breathing. The pediatrician had even observed one of these incidents.

I could only speculate how Mike's four-year-old mind might have been operating: When you don't breathe, you feel weak, dizzy; it's as if you're going to pass out, become unconscious, die. But in his naiveté he could not know that breathing is an autonomic function; when you pass out the body automatically breathes, a built-in survival mechanism. But it is conceivable that Mike surmised that restricting his breathing was a way of killing himself.

Finally, whether out of sheer desperation for attention, or in angry retaliation toward his parents, Mike began to light fires in the house. After the draperies had been charred and a large hole burned in the living room rug, the Harrises at last sought professional help. They apparently had no understanding of Mike's behavior other than that it was "God's will . . . "

Fortunately, the pediatrician sized up the situation, realized that Mike needed to be removed from the home,

and advised the parents that immediate psychiatric treatment was imperative. He referred them to a mental health
center and, after the admission interview two weeks later,
Mike became Merrick State Psychiatric Hospital Patient
No. 65433-CU.

On admission Mike must have been virtually psychotic, his speech a regressive and incoherent word salad,
accompanied by tirelessly choreographed movements: left
arm forward, right arm back, one step forward, one step
back, arms swing out, two steps forward, two steps back,
then right arm forward, left arm back, one step forward,
one step back. . . . During the intake interview Mike was
like a wound up toy, and he totally shunned the group.

After leaving him at the hospital, his parents then completed their abandonment of him. Since his admission they
had never visited and had resisted every effort by the staff to
make contact with them. From the start, Mike had been one
of the few children in the unit who never went home—even
at Christmas, when it was especially tough to be confined to
the hospital.

In the three years since his admission, little had
changed. He always fled from people, particularly adults.
This stemmed partly from an incident that occurred not
long after Mike came to the hospital when a group of aides
cornered him and, holding him down, washed and cut
his hair, which was outlandishly long and matted. Evidently
though, it was an exercise not to be repeated. He had been
like a ferocious little weasel—fighting, biting, and scratch-
ing. And it must have been a sharp reminder of his life at
home because that night Mike had tried to hang himself
with his belt.

About two months after the enforced haircut a teacher

had come upon him in a classroom, snub-nosed, paper-cutting scissors in hand, snipping and sawing huge chunks of his hair, which was growing long again. Ever since, Mike had been allowed to do the job himself as best he could, which explained the uneven straw-blond swatches and cowlicks that gave him the appearance of a short-circuited scarecrow.

On the whole Mike had survived by becoming as self-contained as a turtle. And as he had grown, so had his shell. He never related to the staff or the other children, preferring the company of his own ritualistic gestures and meaningless monologues. He would obey simple commands if only to ensure that adults kept their distance. His antennae were always out sweeping, and if an adult came near, Mike skittered away sidelong like a little beach crab, watching guardedly for any sign of an imminent threat.

His days were spent sitting listlessly in the dayroom, staring out the window, or attending classes but never participating. Every chance he got, he wandered the grounds restlessly like some caged animal and, as Scott had noted, from time to time Mike was seen roaming the hills above the hospital. Occasionally when a belligerent child would pick a fight, Mike would react in a primitive fashion: he would run away if he could, fight if there was no place to run, but never seek protection from an adult.

Over the years various therapists had tried to reach Mike and win his confidence. One had sought to entice him into the play therapy room with bowls of ice cream, his favorite food. But Mike had spurned her attempts. Another therapist, obviously in the throes of frustration, had written that he considered Mike to be "organically paranoid" and hence, "absolutely untreatable."

It was a devastating story. And it all sounded pretty hopeless. Mike had clearly never even had a shot at learning the means and mechanisms of relating to other people. Instead, he was locked into a way of life that was as barren as it was rigid. And, with each passing year, it was becoming more difficult for him to break out of it—or for anyone to break into it.

At home that night I went through my textbooks and notes from psychopathology seminars to review what was known about childhood schizophrenia. The theoretical notions and research materials were familiar, but now they took on added interest when brought to bear on an actual child.

I sifted through a wide variety of explanations about what caused schizophrenia in childhood. Several pointed the finger of blame at the parents, with the most severe indictment directed at the omnipotent and domineering mother who had been observed often enough to have earned a label—the *schizophrenogenic mother*. Literally, one who produces schizophrenia by choking off growth, adaptation, integration. She does this by psychologically whipsawing the child—giving such contradictory messages and inter-actions that no matter what the youngster says or does, he's wrong, and this becomes grounds for vindictive criticism and punishment. It's the classic double-bind, no-win situation.

Other researchers had identified a relentlessly posses-sive type of mother who refuses to nurture the individuality of her child, preferring instead to foster such a smothering and intertwined relationship that the youngster cannot dis-tinguish himself from her. In time, this ego suffocation leads to such a profound degree of dependence that any hint of separation from the mother is generally sufficient to propel the child into an absolute panic, if not psychotic frenzy. From what I could gather from the case history, though, Mike's family did not appear to conform to either profile. The pattern they came closest to was that of the "refrigerator mother" who operates in tandem with an absentee father. Neither provides any form of emotional sustenance to the offspring. These types of parents often neglect even basic physical care: feeding, changing, and bathing are erratic at best. In time such acute rejection and isolation effectively warp the psychological development, leaving the child incapable of experiencing reality in a meaningful and goal-oriented way. The result—a major structural defect in personality.

That explanation matched Mike's situation, along with the solid evidence that persons from families with a higher incidence of schizophrenia are more vulnerable than persons from nonafflicted families. The research had shown that 12 to 14 percent of children with a schizophrenic parent develop the disorder. In cases where both parents have schizophrenia, the probabilities jump to 35 percent. Perhaps there was a predisposing factor; Mike's mother had been hospitalized for emotional problems, although nowhere in the record could I find a reference to her diagnosis.

This research in genetic determinants was also related to various hypotheses that suggested a physiological basis for schizophrenia, that some agent—a biochemical anomaly, a breakdown in the ability of the brain's neurotransmitters to filter and assimilate information, even a vitamin deficiency—was responsible for setting the symptoms in motion.

It was all rather confusing; obviously no one knew for sure. But there could be no doubt about one conclusion: Schizophrenia, especially in its childhood form, is the most devastating of emotional disorders, ravaging the orderly process of growth, wreaking havoc with the most intricate component of humanness—the personality. It severely disrupts that most crucial of developmental tasks, the ability to relate and attach to other human beings.

Parental abuse and neglect play a prominent role, with the hapless child unable to ward off the onslaught of fear, anxiety, and eventual despair. Such psychological torment is exhausting. Finally, in a desperate bid for survival, the child withdraws, slowly throttling his feelings until they gasp, sputter, and ultimately lapse into dormancy.

That is the break with reality, the splitting off, the retreat from others and into oneself, with a progressive reliance upon a reverie of distorted thoughts and fantasies to provide a protective, if highly limited, mode of survival. For Mike, though, even the relative protection offered by his craziness had been insufficient to shield him from the acute pain—so he had sought to end his life. Fortunately that period had passed; with the understanding he had come to with the staff, there were no further suicide attempts. Just three years of apparent oblivion.

I closed my notebook and sat back, staring into space. Here I was in my first professional position, about to take on a patient whose pathology had, so far, consistently defied treatment. And yet, as inexperienced as I was, I still felt confident. More so than was justified, really. Perhaps it was a function of my determination, but . . .

The more I thought about it, the more I sensed some connection with my past. Like Mike, I had been something

of a loner myself, although I had most definitely never
known the privations he had. On the contrary, I had come
from a sensible, caring, middle-class background, growing
up in a suburb of Los Angeles. But I was a kid who was
overwhelmed by the big city—the masses, the noise, the
confusion. My reaction had been to rebel, to go against the
grain. I dropped out of college and then spent the next few
years drifting, ski-bumming the High Sierras in the winter,
migrating in the summer to the surfing beaches of Southern
California.

During those years, I came to understand that the
nomadic existence was a means of escape, a way of protecting my sensitivity. It also allowed me to counter the fear
of what others thought of me. I had felt that I didn't belong,
and so I placed myself on the fringe of society, where there
was much less risk, less pressure to conform. I was even
more comfortable with those on the outer fringe of the
fringe, like the two men who had come to mind when Scott
mentioned working with Mike.

Charlie was a lapsed businessman who lived from day
to day dragging a screen frame over the public beaches
early each morning. Several hours' work usually resulted in
a few dollars' worth of coins and an occasional ring or
watch. He spent the rest of the time drinking muscatel and
reminiscing about a life turned sour. I could listen for hours
to Charlie's rough-and-ready knowledge of the rat race that
he now despised. But I couldn't help but notice the terrible
sadness of his eyes, gleaming at me through puffy slits of
flesh, and separated by an enormously bulbous red nose.

The other extreme case of alienation that I had encountered was Lars. He lived deep in the Sierras in a small
hand-built cabin, where his only company was a pair of

woodchucks. Though Lars was avoided by most of the others who frequented the ski lodge, I knew at the time he wasn't any crazier than I was. He was just one of the most profoundly lonely people I'd ever met and come to befriend. I could still picture the dust-covered, beautifully-made snowshoes he had crafted for his wife, who had left him some twenty years before—a rejection from which he apparently had never recovered.

People like Lars and Charlie touched a deep chord in me. Even then I had tried to understand the twists of fate that accounted for their bad fortune. They seemed so desolate and yet there appeared to be nothing they or anyone else could do about it. That was the way things had turned out for them, as each would have been the first to admit. Yet in my youthful optimism and concern, I kept thinking of alternatives for them, ways that might get them out of their ruinous ruts.

It was also true, as I came to realize, that niggling away in some remote corner of my mind was the fear that what had happened to them could also, given the right circumstances, happen to me. . . .

I spent the next few days sounding out the professional staff who knew Mike, delving for any clues that might suggest a starting point. I first tracked down Jody Fletcher, who was head nurse at Mike's cottage. A small, pretty young woman who laughed easily, she was younger than most head nurses, but I soon understood why she was in charge; what she lacked in age and stature, she made up for in authority.

We were joined by Chuck Benson, a psychiatric aide who had known Mike since his admission three years before. Chuck was a heavily muscled ex-marine in his late thirties whose arms were covered with tattoos. He shook my hand self-consciously and insisted on addressing me as "Doc."

"We were just talking about Mike Harris, Chuck. Maybe there's something you could add," Jody said.

"What do you want to know about him, Doc?" he asked, and I could hear the rasp of a marine drill instructor in his voice. "There's not much to tell—" He glanced at Jody.

"That's true enough," Jody agreed. "We've really drawn a blank on Mike. He's definitely not been one of our success stories. We've tried just about everything to draw him out, but so far he's resisted us. Still, there's an appealing quality about him that makes us sense that if we could just find the right approach, he'd respond."

"What makes you say that?"

"For one thing, it's the way he follows us. You know, it's very unusual for a kid as disturbed as Mike to show any interest at all in other people. I've never seen it happen before to the degree it has with Mike. But the minute we acknowledge he's there, that's it. At first we thought that once he felt he could trust us, he'd relent and let us help him. But it's never happened."

"What kinds of things have been done so far?"

"Oh, over the years different therapists have tried to get him involved in toys or games, stuff like that. But there's never been even a flicker of interest. Most of us have just worked toward gaining his trust by doing little things for him and by not pushing him or making demands. We've come around to allowing him to set his own rules with the hope that eventually he'll initiate some kind of interaction."

"Which, unfortunately, he's never done," said Chuck. "You know, usually a kid will soften up and begin to relate, but Mike's just so closed off he won't even let you come near him—twenty-five feet, that's the limit."

"Not even any of the other kids? No one's ever observed anything like that?"

"Nope, nothing." Chuck shrugged. "From what we've seen, Doc, Mike just doesn't talk or interact on any level except to do what few simple things we ask—take his meds, go to school, meals, things like that. And that's just to get along and avoid being hassled."

"It's an accommodation of sorts," added Jody.

Chuck nodded. "Yeah, and it's worked for him so far. We're deadlocked, and I'm afraid everyone else around here is going to tell you exactly the same thing. . . ."

He was right. Cecile Stevens, Mike's middle-aged teacher, could add only that Mike's time in school was spent staring out the window. "I've made so many attempts to attract his attention through books, drawings, colors—even cartoon movies, which the other kids love. But—" She shrugged. People did a lot of shrugging when it came to Mike.

And then there was Tom Gazarro, Mike's social worker, who had interviewed the parents on the day Mike was admitted. Tom's one-word description of them was "weird!"

"They've never answered my letters, apparently don't have a phone, or else it's unlisted. What it amounts to is that they've simply abandoned Mike, virtually disowned him. They evidently want nothing more to do with him, or with us. It's a damn shame! And it shouldn't be tolerated, but under the circumstances, what do you do?" He paused for a moment. "You know, I could understand that attitude more easily with some of the other kids here; a few of them work pretty hard at alienating the people around them and it takes real grit to put up with them for any length of time. But Mike—well, he just got a bum deal."

The chief psychiatrist, Mark Conable, seemed as baffled as everyone else about Mike. He admitted candidly that all he had been doing was prescribing a maintenance dose of an antipsychotic tranquilizer, and that there had been little change over the years. On a few occasions he'd decreased or discontinued the medications altogether to see what would happen, but Mike then became more overtly psychotic, unable even to get dressed or go to school. Otherwise, Conable's contacts with him had been infrequent, although he too had been followed by Mike from time to time.

What it all came down to was that Mike was as much a mystery to the people who had been around him for years as he was to me.

That first week I also wrote to Mike's parents informing them that I was going to be seeing him in therapy and that I very much needed their assistance in my efforts. Would they please call me—collect. Two weeks later I still had not heard from them, though from what Tom had said that didn't surprise me. I tried once more, sending a follow-up letter saying it was urgent that I talk with them about Mike. There was no response to that either.

In the meantime, Scott was keeping my days busy. He would observe me testing a patient, then meticulously check my scoring of the Wechsler Intelligence Scale for Children and the Rorschach Inkblot Test. Together we would go over the hypotheses I had drawn from them, along with those from the Bender-Gestalt, the Children's Apperception

Test, and the Draw-a-Person Test. Then he would drill me on translating the information into the cohesive psychodynamic description of the child that formed the basis for our treatment recommendations.

Whenever I had a chance, though, I observed Mike from his prescribed distance. What I saw was a grubby little ragamuffin in a misbuttoned faded flannel shirt, patched blue jeans, and tattered sneakers. But under that disheveled veneer was a slender body with the sleek gliding motion of a potential athlete. There was even an odd grace to the ritualized steps he seemed compelled to do throughout the day.

But it was his face that fascinated me. His expression was always the same—a somber, unyielding mask—and I had never encountered one quite like it. His impoverished existence was painfully reflected in the pinched narrowing of his deep-set hazel eyes, the unmistakable constraint in his thin, tightly compressed lips, and the tension of preparedness with which he carried himself. Constantly on guard, alert for danger, he resembled a small, vulnerable creature in a thicket of predators. In many ways Mike seemed old, even wizened, a world-weary eight-year-old.

Finally, I told Scott I was as ready as I would ever be. When he asked me about my therapy plan for Mike, I started out with the notes and ideas I'd been developing. I mentioned the psychoanalyst Bruno Bettelheim, who has written several books advocating love and understanding as the best possible treatment for childhood schizophrenia. Another analyst, Melanie Klein, suggests climbing into the psychotic shell of the youngster and leading him out. "But she doesn't say exactly how to do it . . . " I stole a glance at Scott and retreated to safer territory.

The psychotherapist I had read most avidly was Carl

Rogers. His position is that the success of psychotherapy is dependent upon the attitudes communicated by the therapist; he stresses the importance of empathy—sensing what the disturbed person is feeling—and of accepting that person with unconditional positive regard. Most important, the therapist must be open and guileless. All of these attitudes form the basis for trust, and thus facilitate growth and change. So far, my experience at the university clinic had convinced me that this approach worked. Also, the concepts were consistent with my own view of the nature and worth of human beings. I considered myself to be a "Rogerian"—a client-centered therapist.

Virginia Axline, another psychotherapist who specialized in working with troubled children, had written a book in which she incorporated Rogers' ideas into play therapy, but her approach, as did his, depended upon a certain degree of cooperation.

"And then there's operant conditioning. A lot of people have had success using behavioral techniques in the treatment of schizophrenia. But that's so controlling. You're really just programming the kid, using rewards to train rote behavior. Besides, I'd have to catch Mike in a net to get him hooked on M&Ms or Fruit Loops as reinforcers. I wouldn't know where to start."

Scott nodded. Then he smiled. "You seem to be running out of theorists . . . "

"Not quite. I know she's out of style, but I've always been impressed by the writings of Frieda Fromm-Reichmann. She speaks of how important it is for the therapist to help the person with schizophrenia discover that life with others can be bearable and even rewarding. That there are ways to get along, that people don't have to live in a world of irreality and delusions. Problem is, her neo-analytic approach is also dependent on being able to get near the child." Warming to the task and somewhat impressed with how much information I had memorized, I rattled along, parroting all the wisdom I had gleaned from my readings.

Scott listened, drawing reflectively on his pipe. Finally he raised his hand and I ground to a halt.

"You've got all the jargon down, haven't you? But let's get practical now. What exactly is your plan going to be?"

"I really don't know what will work—or even what approach I should try first. I thought maybe I'd just experiment, cast about."

"Do you think play therapy is feasible with Mike?"

"I doubt it, particularly if I can't get closer to him than twenty-five feet. Besides, others have tried that and no one's gotten to first base."

"So what *are* you going to do?"

"I guess I'll just go over to the cottage and explain to Mike that we're going to be spending some time together and then take it from there. I'll just have to play it by ear."

Scott looked dubious. "That doesn't sound very professional. We usually try for a bit more structure than 'playing it by ear.' What about all that stuff you were quoting from the books a minute ago?"

"I don't know. None of it seems to fit right now. I guess I just won't know until I see how Mike reacts to me."

Scott looked doubly dubious, but then his face relaxed into a rather disconcerting smile. He seemed amused.

"So you're going to wing it. Well, that should prove interesting—for you as well as for Mike."

CHAPTER THREE

THE NEXT AFTERNOON I SET OUT TO SEE MIKE FOR THE first meeting. I was clad in a brown corduroy coat, button-down shirt, striped tie, beige denims, and loafers. The ensemble had been carefully selected to reflect casual professionalism. I had also been cultivating my warmest, most patient tone of voice; a gentle, understanding smile; and a pipe—generally unsmoked, but always available as a suitable prop.

When I reached the cottage door I pushed the buzzer, stepped inside, and within a few moments Chuck, the aide I had talked with a few days earlier, joined me. Together we located Mike in a corner of the dayroom, staring out one of the heavily screened windows. He sensed our approach and darted away.

"Hi, Mike." I poured my most empathetic manner into the two words.

No response.

"Mike, my name is Pat. You've seen me around the hospital—I'm the one who waves at you, remember? And from now on you and I are going to be getting together regularly and doing things. Whatever you want to do, okay?"

Still no response except for Mike's eyes, which swept back and forth from Chuck to me and back again.

I tried again, though already I was beginning to hear strain in my voice. "Mike, is there something you'd like to do with me today?"

From over my shoulder came Chuck's gravelly voice. "Forget it, Doc, he doesn't talk to people."

I glanced back at him and in that instant Mike saw his opportunity. He shot past us, out the dayroom door, and down the hall—as far away as he could go.

"Look, Doc, that kid's been here three years and, like I told you, none of us have ever been able to get him to talk to us, much less come near us. If we want him to go somewhere, into a room or outside, then we tell him it's okay and walk away from the door. That's the deal we have with him. We stay away from him, and he does what we say. It's as simple as that."

I nodded, trying hard to appear to take what he said in stride. One professional to another.

"Okay, let's let him out."

Chuck ambled down the hall, unlocked the door leading outside, and blocked it open. Then he turned to Mike, who was standing near his room, tense and vigilant.

"Okay, Mike, you can go out with the Doc here, but you stick with him and you come back when he tells you to, okay? You understand that, Mike?" Chuck backed away from the open door.

As he slipped toward it, Mike continued to watch us. Then, flashing one quick glance at me, he vanished.

Chuck turned toward me with a shrug of his shoulders.

He'd probably seen a slew of interns like me over the years, fresh out of graduate school, full of newly absorbed facts and ideas, primed with fantasies of rescuing people.

I nodded a thanks to him and walked quickly to the center of the quad; Mike was nowhere to be seen. After searching awhile, I caught a glimpse of a small figure lurking in the bushes near the twenty-foot-high boundary fence. From a measured distance, I talked into the bushes.

"Mike, you can run all day, but we could be doing something that's fun."

The chain link fence rattled, and suddenly Mike emerged on the other side of it. He turned abruptly then, and began to walk along a narrow, overgrown path leading into the hills.

Scrambling through the bushes, I discovered a well-concealed hole, just large enough for a person to squeeze through. I eased into the opening, hooking my coat in the process, and by the time I clambered through, Mike was nearly out of sight. Half running, I chased him up the slope. When I was about fifty feet behind him, though, he began to walk faster, so I dropped back, panting and out of breath, allowing him to set the pace. He stayed well ahead of me, every so often turning to be sure I was keeping my distance.

After another fifteen minutes or so of climbing, the trail broke out onto a plateau covered by a well-maintained citrus grove. Mike ran immediately to the nearest tree, picked a large lemon, and began to eat it—skin and all.

I couldn't believe it! Even from where I stood, my mouth puckered in protest. Yet Mike's expression had not changed. How could he *do that?!* And then it occurred to me that the fruit was probably sprayed. I shouted to him to stop, that the lemons might be poisonous and they might make him sick.

Mike kept chewing.

I moved in to take it away, but he was too quick and scuttled off before I was even close. Changing my strategy, trying for a more authoritarian voice, I said,

"Give me that lemon!"

Mike continued to take huge bites, all the time keeping a wary eye on me.

"Look, we don't want you to be sick, do we?"

In response, he stuffed the last wedge of lemon into his mouth, reached up, and plucked off another.

As he devoured the second lemon, I sagged against a tree. What the hell would Carl Rogers do in a spot like this, I thought. Fantasies began running through my mind of my first patient becoming critically ill, maybe even dying. How would I explain to Scott that Mike had eaten a bunch of pesticide-coated lemons up at the citrus orchard and now they were (a) pumping his stomach, (b) doing an autopsy on him, (c) considering filing negligence charges against me, (d) all of the above . . .

Meanwhile, I watched Mike pick yet another lemon. This time, eating it slowly and calmly, he turned and started up the trail again, then stopped to look back at me. I obediently followed.

That's when it struck me that Mike, unable to tell me what he wanted to do, was trying to show me—he wanted to hike. We climbed on, eventually reaching a line of rocks that marked the top of the ridge.

Oblivious of me, Mike chanted some unintelligible words and sidestepped with a swaying motion. Perhaps, I thought, expressing his satisfaction at reaching the crest. Or maybe that was just my projection—I had hardly anticipated this kind of treatment situation.

As he rocked slowly, gazing out over the valley, I realized that he must have come here many times before. Sitting down on a small boulder, he continued the swaying motion, totally absorbed in whatever was going on inside his head.

I commented on the beauty of the spot and thanked him for letting me tag along, but he ignored me. Finally we both sat in silence—the required twenty-five feet apart—and listened to the wind.

As we trudged back, my loafers dusty and scratched, my coat dangling from my shoulder, I had to smile at how ill-prepared I had been. Mike ran on ahead, his nonsensical singsong drifting back to me. Occasionally the words sounded familiar, but they were so looped and jumbled together as to defy interpretation.

Other times his mutterings were just that: "Ka-ka-jah-bah-bow-boooo-gah-bah-jah-kaaaa." The most frequent version was a repetitious, lilting hum, like the chant of a mantra:

"Ahooooooommmm-ahooooooooooommmm-*ahooo-oooooooommmmmmmm* . . ."

From time to time Mike turned to check the distance between us. Perhaps he was establishing with me the same understanding he had with the aides and nurses: If you come no closer, I won't run away.

When Mike reached the cottage, he rang the bell and disappeared inside before I had a chance to say anything to him. I was beat—in more ways than one—and with a desultory wave to Chuck, I turned and hobbled slowly back to my office.

Two days later I was ready to give it another go. It was a beautiful, warm summer day and this time I was prepared—I had exchanged my suit for hiking boots and Levi's. Mike was in the dayroom again, rocking back and forth and staring out the window, arms clasped around his knees.

"Hi, Mike. How about another hike today?"

I was standing far enough away so that I wouldn't startle him, and was concentrating so hard on him that I was unaware of anyone else in the room. Suddenly a number of other children materialized at my side, jumping up and down and pulling on my sleeve.

"Me too, me too!" . . . "I wanna go on a hike!" . . . "Take me, too!"

I hastily explained that Mike and I were going to be seeing each other regularly and doing things together. Just as they did with their social workers or with one of the doctors.

"Yeah, but they never take *us* on hikes!"

"Well, ask them to sometime. I'm sure they'd take you if they knew you really wanted to go." I was more sure I'd hear about this later from the staff.

During all this Mike had continued to stare intently out the window.

"C'mon, Mike, let's go."

Without a glance in my direction, he slid from his chair and walked toward the outside door. I followed, amazed that he could appear so withdrawn and yet respond immediately when he wanted to. Obviously there were times when

he was attuned, well in touch with reality. What was baf-
fling was that it was impossible to tell from his expression or
posture when he was out of contact. And although it was
evident that he was alert to certain things going on around
him, could comprehend at least some of what others said
to him, he had apparently lost, or perhaps never mastered,
the ability to communicate with them in return.

We left the cottage, Mike setting a brisk pace as he
headed directly for the hole in the fence, again ignoring my
attempts at long-range conversation. After the first hike, I
had checked with the rancher, who assured me that the
lemons in the orchard were safe. In fact, he had often seen
Mike walking through the grove, calmly chewing a lemon.

As before, Mike reached the summit well ahead of me.
When I cleared the last rise, he was already perched on the
same rock as the last time, swaying gently, lips moving in
some silent conversation.

Going as close as I dared, I tried repeatedly to elicit an
intelligible response, or at least some reaction, but none
was forthcoming. Apparently he'd convinced himself that
he had nothing to fear from me, and now was behaving as
though I weren't there. His solitariness remained absolute.

For some time we sat in silence. It was a relief to get
away from the Children's Unit with its institutional routine.
The incessant noise and confusion were beginning to wear
on me. Here the air was sweet, the landscape spacious, the
rolling hills giving way to the rows of citrus trees that
stretched across the valley. Recalling my own years in the
mountains, I could well understand why Mike liked to visit
this spot.

It intrigued me that there was no mention of these hikes
in the nursing notes. How long had Mike been coming up

here? Was this a recent interest, or something he had been doing for a long time? I glanced at my watch and realized I had to be in a staff meeting in forty-five minutes.

"Time to go back, Mike."

Remarkably, he looked over at me. For a moment his face relaxed slightly and I thought I caught a brief glimpse of the little eight-year-old who was under the layers of wariness and isolation. Then the curtain dropped again, the fixed expression returned, and he was on his feet, nimbly picking his way along the rocky path.

As usual Mike was far ahead of me all the way back, ringing the bell and disappearing into the building as I rounded the corner. I managed to call, "Bye, Mike. See you Monday," as the door closed behind him.

That night I wondered whether I had actually seen up in the hills what I thought I had. Maybe his momentary unguardedness was just wishful thinking on my part; I wasn't sure. By now I wanted so much to reach him.

But that's how it began, the series of skirmishes and truces that were to characterize the relationship between the novice therapist and his veteran opponent.

CHAPTER FOUR

THE NEXT SEVERAL MONTHS WERE VIRTUALLY A STANDOFF.
My fantasy of Mike's responding dramatically to my
warmth and sincerity soon crumbled as the forces of unconditional positive regard, acceptance, and empathy did
not liberate him, did not open the world of reality to him.

Repetition compressed time to the point where it felt as
if I had been seeing Mike forever, each meeting a carbon
copy of the previous one. Several times a week I would
dutifully appear at the cottage after Mike was out of school,
prop the door open while he sidled out, and then follow
after him, slipping through the familiar hole in the fence
and up into the high country. But I enjoyed it anyway, even
though there was never any progress. It was therapeutic for
me just to get away, to smell the fresh, pungent sage and
then, from the top of the hill, to stare out toward the gray
haze of the channel islands.

It took me back to my days on the ski patrol at Mam-
moth Mountain. There I had prized the first runs of the crisp
mornings when I would often sweep to a stop and look

back, contemplating the meandering doodle of curves I had inscribed on the light, fresh powder. I recalled again the freedom and exquisite beauty, the massive stillness of the frosted mountain broken only by the soft running of skis. During those aimless years, that tranquillity alone had been enough. Now it seemed a long time ago . . .

It was impossible to know how Mike regarded what we did. Frequently he hiked along the trail silently and mechanically, looking either straight ahead or down. If I called his attention to a swooping hawk or a dart-tongued lizard, he ignored me. At other times he catapulted into craziness. He would become echolalic, his voice a shrill monotone as he repeated sounds to himself, reeled off strings of nonsense syllables, or phrased sentences that had psychotic overtones.

One day just outside the fence, Mike began to slap one hand with the other and to shriek: "Mi-koe baahd boy! . . . Mi-koe BAAHD BOY!"

At first, because of his peculiar pronunciation, I couldn't understand him, but after a time it dawned on me that he was saying bad—"Michael is a *bad* boy!" And at that point I had to agree with him. The strident babbling was beginning to set my teeth on edge, and I couldn't fathom what had precipitated the outburst. I tried to counteract his frenzy by declaring, "Michael is a *good* boy. Michael is my friend."

It was a pretty absurd spectacle, a boy and a man twenty-five feet apart, each shouting opposing statements over and over as though baying to the gods, while they climbed single file into the hills. If I needed anything to underscore my sense of futility, this exchange of contradictory and repetitive messages certainly did the trick. Moreover, nothing seemed to subdue him; the ranting continued until we reached the crest. By that time Mike's voice was a rasping wheeze. Mine wasn't much better. The contest had gone on for nearly half an hour—and then the wailing ceased as abruptly as it had begun.

I wondered where Mike could have picked up the phrase, and whether it was connected to some recent event. But when I inquired later, none of the aides or nurses or his teacher recalled saying anything like that to him.

I related the incident to Scott. He said that Mike's verbal seizure was fairly typical of kids like him, that in all likelihood this was material that had been stored in his memory for years, probably going back to when he was still living with his parents. It would doubtless continue to emerge sporadically.

I was moved by the thought that these were the words he remembered most from his early childhood. It was another moment when I sensed the child inside the patient, and I redoubled my determination to help him.

There were other times during those first months when I couldn't relate to Mike's behavior at all. For example, his movements and posture would become stiff, his stride resembling that of a blue heron. He would pick up one leg and step rigidly forward, appearing to freeze in space while he carefully scanned the ground before completing the step. These gestures had a ceremonial, superstitious quality to them, as if he had taken seriously the sidewalk game of "step on a crack—break your mother's back." Once begun, Mike seemed compelled to continue this way of walking as though to ward off some terrible thing that might happen if he stopped, or perhaps only to assure some degree of order to a world that he felt was threatening to overwhelm him.

His most frequent mode of ritualistic behavior was to spin in slow circles, hands outstretched, humming monotonically and rocking to and fro like a slow-motion disco dancer. I called these movements his solitary dance, an eerie blend of self-stimulation and magical symbolism, its source unknown and perhaps inexplicable.

One day I noticed that Mike's tennis shoes were completely worn out. I mentioned this to Scott and he suggested checking the donated items at the hospital's Clothes Corner. I did and was elated to discover three pairs of children's hiking boots that might fit. That afternoon I took them to the cottage and set them on the lawn near the door. When Mike came out, I pointed to them and urged him to try them on.

After hesitating a few moments he approached them, staring suspiciously while I kept my distance and awaited his verdict. At first I thought he was going to reject them all; but then, selecting the nicest pair, he tentatively shoved his feet into them. Fortunately they seemed to fit, and he clomped around looking at them and scuffing the toes against the ground. Then he mumbled something and charged off toward the fence without bothering to see if I would follow.

As we climbed to the crest of the ridge, Mike kept stopping to check his boots. Perhaps, I thought, to be sure they were still there. Several times he also loosened the laces, adjusted the tongue, and painstakingly retied them. I watched, fascinated. Mike's method of tying his laces was quite involved—an intricate series of knots that ran right to the end. When he was finished it looked like a pigtail—obviously a system that he had devised himself.

His behavior toward me remained the same, but from

then on Mike wore his boots everywhere, even on days we wouldn't be hiking. I took it as a sign of something positive, a straw to prop up my morale.

Another incident occurred about the same time. As we were returning from the hills one afternoon, I asked Mike if he would like an ice cream cone.

As usual, he didn't respond directly; he simply veered around and marched toward the canteen. I followed, amazed as always by the awareness that coexisted with his isolation. Because he was so noncommunicative, one could easily overlook how adaptive he was, how much on top of things he was in his own way. But I wondered whether he would be willing to enter the canteen with me.

When Mike reached the building he stepped cautiously inside, pausing near the door to check out the room. Then, with a glance that clearly indicated I should stay away, he walked up to the counter and pointed mutely to the container of chocolate ice cream.

He nodded tersely when the counterman held up a large cone, his eyes tracking every move as the man scooped out the ice cream and pressed it into the cone. The man said something and laughed but Mike did not respond, keeping his eyes firmly fastened on the cone. Reaching back into the freezer, the man added another generous dollop. He smiled, asked Mike his name, while holding the cone tantalizingly out of his reach. Mike suddenly seemed on the verge of panic, anxiety clearly etched on his face. Seeing this, the man relented, set the cone on the counter, and stepped back. Mike promptly snatched it and fled the room.

"He's a strange one, that kid," the counterman said, shaking his head. "But then, out here I guess they all are, aren't they? Sure is rough when they're that young."

"Yeah," I agreed. "Mike's a very lonely and frightened kid."

"Too bad," he said, still shaking his head. "Makes you wonder what happened to him, don't it? Mike's his name, huh? I'll remember that."

"By the way, thanks for giving him a little extra. Even though he couldn't say anything, I'm sure he appreciated it."

"Oh, I do it for all the kids. Geez, you know, you feel so sorry for them, that young and all, and stuck in this place . . ."

I nodded. I did indeed know how he felt.

As I left the canteen, though, I was encouraged. Another tiny glimmer of hope. Mike had again acknowledged something I had said and had even allowed me to do something for him by accepting my offer of an ice cream cone. And in the process he had inadvertently revealed that he *was* listening to me—at times, anyway—and that he could understand and relate to me in his own constricted way.

Still, the silences and distances between us were frustrating, to say the least. By nature we are communicative creatures, and being with someone as intensively as I was with Mike, without a response from him for weeks at a time, made me feel so futile. Our relationship seemed unreal at times. As, indeed, it was. Although Mike tolerated me, we hardly had what could be considered a reciprocal relationship. And the frustration was building; after three months I was impatient for results.

It was Scott who kept me glued together during that period. Several times a week I would sprawl in the big leather chair next to his desk and, more often than not, recount my latest stalemate with Mike. One day he had had enough of my glumness and let me have it with both barrels.

"Beginning therapists like you are always in such a hurry, always expecting immediate success. You're so ingrained with the American ethic of quick results for little effort—of instant change when it suits you—that you can't stand the thought of little or no progress, no overnight success stories like in the movies!

"It takes *time* to build a relationship, Patrick, to gain an understanding of the patient's psychodynamics, to earn his trust. It's taken little Mike eight years to get to where he is now. How can you expect him to change it all in a few months? Especially when you're clambering over the mountainside for only four or five hours out of each week? If it were truly that simple, don't you think someone around here would've stumbled on that solution and helped Mike long ago?"

Still, in spite of Scott's lecture, I was rapidly approaching my wits' end. Three months in the trenches were getting to me. All that time I had been chasing that kid, and he still wouldn't come a jot closer, talk to me, or for that matter, even recognize that I was any different from one of the rocks he liked to rest on. Except that he'd get close to *them* . . .

"Well, at least you're getting into shape," Scott commented.

"I'm afraid that little guy has really got my number, but good."

"Want to give up? Try one of the other kids? Lots of other possibilities around here—"

"Of course not! I'm just getting started. I can be just as stubborn . . . no, *more* stubborn, than Mike. But what I haven't been able to figure out yet is how to break the pattern—how to get him to relate to me."

"Maybe it's time you went back to square one."

"What do you mean?"

"Perhaps you should begin to put some of your knowledge of psychology to use: instead of allowing Mike to call all the shots, you start calling some of them."

"I still don't follow, Scott. I've been trying to do that all along, and I can't think of any other way than I've already tried."

"What exactly have you been doing up to this point?"

"Well, I've been trying to do what Rogers advocates —provide unconditional positive regard, acceptance, empathy. The emotional symptoms and distress are supposed to subside as the innate forces within the person strive for psychological balance. That's the theory, anyway. And it seems to work for Rogers . . . "

Scott smiled. "Have you seen any evidence that it's working with Mike?"

"No, not really. Maybe a look from him here and there, but I can't even be absolutely sure of that, especially at a distance of twenty-five feet."

"Okay, now. Are you ready to consider the notion that perhaps one theoretical approach is just not enough to cover all therapeutic situations? That there is no one method of therapy that is going to be applicable to every single patient we encounter?"

"I suppose." It was a grudging admission for me. Scott had broached the subject before, without much success.

"Boy, you're not kidding when you say you're stubborn! Patrick, do yourself a favor and ease up a bit. You've admitted that several months of work with Mike have gone nowhere, so you've got nothing to lose by considering other possibilities, have you?"

"I'm not sure. What do you have in mind?"

"You know how I feel about Rogers' approach. It's an excellent attitude to have toward the people you work with, but there may be some patients who need much more than an interested, supportive listener. I suspect Mike is one of them." Scott gave me a wry smile. "As a fellow humanist I can wholeheartedly agree with the sentiments behind Rogers' ideas, the fact that his concepts are based upon a deep respect for the person and his or her life situation, and that the therapeutic relationship is then constructed upon that premise. But remember, self theory falls far short of being a universal explanation of human behavior."

"What's the alternative, then?" I said, sensing what was coming. "You don't think behaviorism is the answer, do you?"

"Not entirely. But the principles of learning and conditioning have been demonstrated very nicely in studies, especially those by B. F. Skinner. Behaviorism does have its uses and some very good techniques. In spite of what you might think. Of course, it has its limits of usefulness, too, like any other theory. But we know that in certain situations positive and negative reinforcement work extremely well in changing specific types of behavior patterns. So you don't want to disregard learning theory simply because it may be anathema to your humanistic notions.

"Psychoanalysis, too. Many of Freud's concepts—such as the unconscious, the defenses—have certainly withstood the test of time. The empirical data may not have supported some of the major hypotheses of his theory, but the fact remains that many of the psychodynamic constructs, as well as the therapeutic techniques, have proven extremely useful."

"Scott, it's our same old argument!" I broke in. "I'm a dyed-in-the-wool humanist because I can't buy either the behavioristic view of people as mechanized creatures of reflex or the analysts' notions of unconscious motivation, that behavior is ruled by base instincts. I really believe in the integrity of the individual, and that each person has a choice. *Anyway,* I'm familiar with the principles of the various theories you've mentioned—that's the easy part. The problem is that I can't apply the techniques of *any* of these theories to a little buzz bomb named Michael Harris who runs up and down hills like a mountain goat and won't let me near him!"

"All right," retorted Scott. "The problem is that you have yourself prematurely committed. There are no absolute applications of any of the theories yet—that's why they're still theories. Psychology as a science is, to put it mildly, in diapers. We have a lot of promising leads, some well-conceived studies, some good data, and the start of a body of knowledge. But we are a long way from fully understanding human behavior, much less predicting it with one-hundred-percent accuracy."

"That's for sure. I'm beginning to wonder why I spent so much time in graduate school."

"Well, it's not as hopeless as it may sound. But when you make the jump from the rudiments of science to applied work you have to stay loose, flexible, and accept the fact that you're not always going to be perfectly on target. What the theoretical framework does is increase your chances; it allows you to be objective, to plan, even to predict what *should* happen during the course of psychotherapy. What I'm advocating you do with Mike—with anyone you work with professionally—is concentrate on understanding him and assessing the situation. And be open to using any of the theories that might seem appropriate. So when you first start working with a person, begin by picking out the theory that seems to fit the individual's dilemma best, whether that theory is called self, behaviorism, psychoanalysis, whatever. Use those explanations, but be ready to look elsewhere when they don't seem to account for what's going on. Or when there doesn't seem to be any progress. Stay loose, flexible, open to anything.

"That's what sets true professionals apart: they draw upon their knowledge of science, using their skills to objectively evaluate what is needed, and then they choose a course of action. It's rarely very clear precisely what that should be; sometimes several treatment alternatives would be appropriate. One simply has to make a choice and, if things don't work out, be prepared to switch to another approach.

"And remember, Pat, all the while the patient may very well sense what is best: the Wisdom of the Mind, if you will. Some people, for example, *need* to dig back into the trauma of their formative years and work through unresolved issues and long-buried troublesome feelings—as the psychoanalysts advocate—while others simply blot out the past and deal with learning a more adaptive style of living that is future-oriented. More along the lines of a behavioral approach. But most, the majority I would say, want a combination. You have to learn to mold yourself, to shape yourself to whatever will best help your patient—an accommodation between what *you* sense they need, and what you think *they* sense they need, and what therapeutic approach will be most suitable for that purpose."

I was shaking my head by this time, but Scott pressed on.

"What I'm suggesting therefore, Pat, is that you be more eclectic. Be aware of the value of trying different things instead of being locked into one theory and approach. Mix a little Rogers with some Skinner and maybe add a dash of Freud. Okay?"

"At best I *think* I see what you're getting at, Scott. But I still don't see how using a goulash of theories and techniques is going to help me know what to do with my particular little id kid."

Scott grinned his roguish smile and leaned back, drawing long and thoughtfully on his pipe. When the last thin wisp had emerged, he watched it gyrate toward the ceiling and then he turned to me.

"You like challenges—that's another one for you. Think about what I've said, then try to put it to use."

CHAPTER FIVE

So I HAD TO COME UP WITH ANOTHER PLAN, THE SOONER the better. And then one afternoon a notice appeared on the department bulletin board. Ivar Lovaas, a UCLA psychologist, was scheduled to present a workshop on developments in the treatment of childhood schizophrenia and autism. I knew that Lovaas was a behaviorist who for some time had claimed considerable success in using operant conditioning techniques with severely disturbed children, but that was all I knew about him.

Scott encouraged me to attend, saying, "What have you got to lose?"

Very little, I had to admit. At this point I was willing to listen to anyone, try anything.

Lovaas showed filmed accounts of the treatment program he had devised for schizophrenic and autistic children. All were extreme cases, exhibiting a wide range of self-stimulating behaviors that precluded interaction with others— gazing at light through flapping hands, being mesmerized by spinning objects, or parroting nonsensical speech in an echolalic fashion. In each case specific conditions were set up whereby the child had to produce an appropriate form and level of performance. Using a variety of rewards or "primary reinforcers," the therapist taught simple words, initiated cooperative play, encouraged personal hygiene habits. The idea was that the youngster performed some act —pulled a wagon with another child in it, identified his nose, buttoned a button—and was immediately rewarded with food, especially candy, and "secondary reinforcers" such as the therapist's emphatic *"Goooood!"* accompanied by a smile and a nod. A toothy Lovaas, with his Norwegian accent, managed to string out the word "good" until it was almost an aria. After a short time the child made the connection between the pleasurable reward and the smiling therapist who provided it. The systematic creation of a new behavior pattern also had an unexpected and remarkable side effect: the psychotic mannerisms began to drop away.

More drastic measures were called for with children who engaged in self-stimulating and autistic behaviors. Negative reinforcement could be a sharp "No!," a painful slap, a squirt of lemon juice, and sometimes physical restraints. On occasion, mild electric shocks were used to break up physically self-destructive behavior such as self-hitting and self-biting.

A particularly striking example of this involved a four-year-old girl who for over a year had been gouging her arm with her teeth. Every conventional approach had been tried —including a plaster cast and a pint-sized straitjacket. But as soon as she had access to her arm, the biting resumed. With her arm ulcerated once again, electric shock was applied to teach the child that every time she hurt herself, she could expect an unpleasant jolt. Now the inflicted pain was no longer under her control, and almost immediately the procedure began to "shape" her behavior as she understood the link between injuring herself and the extremely aversive electric shock. Within three weeks the self-mutilation was eliminated—or "extinguished," as the behaviorists say.

Lovaas maintained that all of these intrusive methods, delivered in a consistent fashion, offered the best chance of success in counteracting long-standing psychotic and self-destructive behavior patterns.

I had to agree. It was evident that these techniques had brought about some remarkable changes. Without exception, the before-and-after films were very impressive, showing child after child coming around under the uniform, systematic treatment. And the whole process took only weeks. A sharp contrast to the time needed by the more traditional therapeutic approaches. As Lovaas made clear, the children still had a long way to go, but they were unquestionably more amenable to treatment than they had been before.

I returned from the presentation intrigued by what I had seen, excited by the implications, but also troubled. I couldn't help but compare their success to the absolute frustration I was feeling after months of sparring with Mike. On the other hand, learning theory had always seemed to me too remote, too dehumanizing. Fine for pigeons and rats, but too manipulative and unfeeling for human beings. But I couldn't deny that the techniques appeared to have an amazing effect on children very much like Mike.

And when I began to analyze the interaction between Mike and me in terms of Lovaas's ideology, it became very clear who was getting all the positive reinforcement: Mike was going hiking, having ice cream cones, and doing generally what he wanted to do, all the while forcing me to go by the rules he had established. And it was just as evident who was getting all the negative reinforcement: I was still no closer to Mike, there had been no change in his overall behavior, and nothing to indicate that I was learning to be an effective therapist. No wonder I was frustrated. All my idealistic notions and rescue fantasies were being "extinguished," thwarted by an eight-year-old boy who had done a beautiful job of "shaping" my behavior.

Still, there remained, for me, certain ideological and personal problems with behavior therapy. In particular, the emphasis on minimizing, virtually eliminating, the trusting relationship between therapist and patient—and substituting one that seemed more like that between a trainer and an animal—was completely counter to my training and philosophy. And I was bothered by the aversive procedures and the use of punishment. Shouting "No!" at Mike, or if he were to hit himself during one of his "bad boy" episodes, conceivably having to shock him—all of this seemed terribly insensitive and went against everything I believed in.

I was becoming a psychotherapist to help people, not to inflict physical pain on top of psychological pain. I wanted him to learn how to enjoy closeness, and that seemed a strange way to do it. I just couldn't imagine how Mike, or any child for that matter, would ever be able to trust the adult who zapped him like that. If an association were made between candy and the therapist who gave it, would not just as strong an association be made between the therapist and the shock he delivered? If negative reinforcement were used at all, it needed to be somehow combined with reward. Was there a way of doing that?

The more I thought about it, the more I realized that my resistance to these methods was deeply embedded in my own temperament and background, as was my decision to work with Mike in the first place. My convictions were also closely linked with the personal changes that had brought me out of the wilderness of my own solitude.

Soon after I had decided to return to college, I landed a job as a playground director at a school for blind children. There I worked closely with some twelve youngsters, helped them to build models, took them on trips to the zoo and the park, even managed to produce a circus with them. Nothing in my life until then matched driving down a busy city boulevard with a carload of inquisitive blind children who kept calling out, "What's that noise?" . . . "Why did you slow down?" . . . "Is that a bus?" . . . "When's the tunnel?" . . . And when we reached the tunnel, they would recognize the change in light and a chorus of voices would exclaim, "Tunnel. TUN-NELLLLL!"

The children's adaptiveness to their handicap, and in some cases several handicaps, continually moved me. They were so venturesome, appreciative, and positive that it was a joy to be around them and to share things with them. For the first time in my life I felt I was doing something that was indisputably worthwhile, and it was evident to me that I needed and responded to them as much as they needed and responded to me. Helping people seemed to bring out the best in me, the most confident and purposeful side of my character.

From that revelation evolved a sense of direction that led me back to college and a psychology major. That was how I met Dr. Warfield, who became my adviser. He encouraged me to become a psychologist and indelibly exemplified for me just what it meant to be a psychotherapist.

The most remarkable illustration of Dr. Warfield's skill was provided the first time he took our undergraduate class to visit a nearby mental hospital. We assembled in the one-way observation room where he first briefed us about the different people he'd be interviewing and related their diagnoses to concepts we had studied.

When Dr. Warfield and the first patient entered the group therapy room on the other side of the one-way glass, we were all struck by a dramatic change in him. Gone were his classroom antics; his theatrical lecture style was replaced by a quiet voice and gentle manner. He communicated empathy that reached even the most disorganized and delusional patients, and then coaxed each of them down his or her particular path to reality.

The last one was an attractive woman in her mid-thirties. Her expressive Mediterranean face oozed boredom and derision as she sat chain-smoking and ignoring Dr. Warfield's comments. But her taut expression, coupled with the jerky gestures as she tapped ashes or ground stubs into an ashtray, betrayed an underlying vortex of rage.

Finally the strain became too much and she exploded in a torrent of lurid curses and obscenities that shocked our small group. I had never seen or heard such vehemence—at one point I thought she might even attack Dr. Warfield. But he took it calmly and his voice remained soothing and accepting. The woman tried to light a cigarette, but her hands were shaking so badly that she couldn't. Dr. Warfield lit one for her, then sat back in silence while she regained her composure. Suddenly she broke down in waves of sobbing: "I don't know what came over me, Doctor. I just can't control these feelings any longer—they *haunt* me." Then she slowly began to share the anxieties and fears that were tormenting her. Dr. Warfield skillfully drew her out, gaining her trust with his supportive gentleness. It was the most remarkable performance I'd ever witnessed, and it had remained until now as the main model for what I wanted to do as a therapist.

My quandary now was whether there might be a middle ground for me somewhere between the humanistic concerns of the self theorist and the harsh logistics of the behaviorists. The more I thought about it, the more certain I became that even if the theories themselves were intellectually incompatible, they could share equal time in a practical sense. All it would take would be a little bending of the techniques to fit the situation.

It wouldn't be a very elegant approach—the kind that made for sophisticated scientific presentations—but if it worked, who cared? And if it didn't, I'd just have to come up with another angle. It was at least worth a try. With some chagrin, I realized that I had come around to precisely what Scott had been suggesting: Be flexible. . . . Pick and choose. . . . Anything that might work with a youngster—with anyone—is fair game. . . .

In the previous four months Mike's and my routine had been fairly well established. I would go up to the cottage after school, find Mike, and we would set off on a hike or a walk around the hospital grounds, with an occasional stop at the canteen for a treat.

But at our next session, as Mike stood poised, waiting for me to open the door so he could catapult himself out, I put up my hand and motioned him into the empty dayroom.

He backed in, eyeing me, keeping as much distance between us as he could.

"Mike, I'd like to try something different from now on. Each time I come, I want you to tell me what you want to do. Okay?"

Silence.

"You look as if you're ready for a hike today, so before we go, I'd like you to tell me that. Say 'hike.' Okay? Do you think you can say that for me? 'Hike.'"

Mike sat across the room, his face cupped in his hands, staring out the window. There was no indication that he had heard me, but I knew he had.

I tried again. "Mike, all you have to say is 'hike.' Then we'll leave right away."

No response.

I slowed it down, enunciating clearly. "Mike, look at me. Say it like this: 'Hiii-ka.' That's all you have to say, Mike. Then we'll go. 'Hiii-ka.'"

Mike turned and looked at me, his face expressionless. Then he swung halfway around and gazed impassively out the window again. His face seemed to become more set then, and I wondered how he was interpreting the new condition—as punishment, rejection, an unreasonable demand, a trick? There was no way to tell, but I was determined to wait it out, to see what his reaction would be.

We sat for fifteen minutes. Every now and then I would repeat what he had to say, but Mike paid no attention. He had retreated to somewhere deep inside himself. Finally I decided to tantalize him a bit to see if I could provoke a response.

"You know, Mike, we're missing a beautiful afternoon of hiking; I bet we could see clear across the valley, maybe even see the ocean today. C'mon, let's get out of this crummy cottage for a while, and get away from the hospital. Those lemons up in the orchard are really tasty. One would taste *soooooo* good while you're sitting on your favorite rock at the top of the hill, wouldn't it? C'mon, Mike, all you have to do is say 'hike.' That's not so hard, is it?"

Silence. Mike continued to stare remotely out the window.

Another five minutes dragged by, then ten. Maybe this wasn't going to work after all. Lovaas had sometimes used punishment to force interaction in such a situation, but I had elected to try a more positive approach. Still, if Mike didn't want to hike badly enough . . . maybe it was too much to expect of him. Asking him to speak to me was a big step. Perhaps I should have tried for something easier initially.

Thirty minutes had now passed. I gave it one more try. "Mike, it really is a super day out there." I stood up as if I were about to leave. "Look at me, Mike. Say 'hike.' That's all. C'mon, just try it."

When there was still no reaction, I sat down again, prepared to wait the rest of the afternoon if necessary while I pondered my next tactic. Sometime later I was about to repeat my instructions when I noticed a very slight shift in Mike's shoulders.

Then, with a distinct sigh, his towhead swung in my direction and he stammered a couple of barely audible, unintelligible words.

"What was that, Mike? I'm sorry, I couldn't hear you. Please say it a little louder."

Several more moments passed in silence; then, staring at the floor, he said in a subdued but discernible tone something that sounded like, "Hi dugfahs."

Because of his odd enunciation, it was very difficult to understand what he was saying. It sounded, though, like "Hike" something. What could he be saying? Hike what?

At the moment it didn't matter; it was close enough.

"That's great, buddy! I knew you could do it! That was very, *very good*. Okay, you lead the way!" I smiled and nodded enthusiastically, the pent-up positive reinforcers tumbling out.

Once out the door, Mike was off like a wild mustang. We hiked the rest of the afternoon, but although I watched for a reaction—possibly even a repetition of the words—there was nothing different in his manner. He seemed to have completely forgotten our earlier confrontation. Later, as he disappeared through the door of the cottage, I praised him one last time for talking to me, hoping that it would carry over to the next day.

I went immediately to tell Scott the news. Charging into his office, grubby and bedraggled, I found him on the phone. When he saw me he couldn't help but chuckle. Hanging up the receiver, he said, "You look like the proverbial cat—"

"I got two words out of him! One I understood—'hike' —but the other I couldn't make out. He held out a long time and I was just about to give up when he finally came through! I can't wait to see what happens tomorrow . . . "

"Sounds like a start. But remember—be patient. And don't expect too much."

The next day I had changed into my hiking clothes and was waiting for Mike at the cottage when he returned from school. I ordinarily wouldn't have seen him again until later in the week, but I couldn't wait that long. He seemed unusually reluctant to follow me into the dayroom; if possible, he was more withdrawn and hunched over than ever. He chose the same chair that he had sat in the day before and resumed his familiar staring out the window. So we would have the dayroom to ourselves again, I locked the door behind us and then turned to Mike.

"Okay, shall we decide what to do today? If you want to go hiking again, tell me like you did yesterday. Just say 'hike.'"

We sat in silence for several minutes and then, as I began to think I should repeat my instructions, Mike's lips moved as if in rehearsal. Then he whispered, "Hi," and the elusive word again.

"Mike, please speak a little louder—I can't quite hear what it is you want to do."

"Hi dugfahs."

"Try it once more, Mike. Say the whole word. 'Hiii-ka.'"

For a few tense moments I was afraid he'd clam up again, but at last he muttered, "Hike dugfahs."

"Good, Mike! Great! You said it right that time. That's just fine. I'm really glad you could tell me what you want to do. Going for a hike—" and here I paused, trying to approximate what he had said, "—'dugfahs' is fine with me, too. Let's go!"

Over the next several meetings, Mike quickly adapted to saying the required words on cue. I couldn't believe it. He was being so cooperative that a couple of weeks later, when we were cutting back to the Children's Unit by way of the canteen, I decided to try for a little more.

"Mike, if you want to stop for a Coke or an ice cream

cone, we can. All you have to do is say, 'I want Coke' or
'I want ice cream.'"

Mike acted as if he hadn't heard me, but when we
passed directly behind the canteen, he looked over longingly. So did I. After the dryness and dust of the hike it
seemed like an oasis. He slowed, obviously undergoing an
intense internal battle. Finally he stopped, scuffing his feet
in the dirt, head down. His voice barely carried back to me.

"Geh Coooke."

Two words. I decided to push my luck. "Almost, Mike.
Now say, 'I . . . want . . . Coke.'"

The familiar faraway look returned. Then he repeated,
"Geh-Coooke-now! GehCOOOKENOWWW!" His voice
became an insistent yowl.

I stood my ground. "No, Mike. Say, 'I . . . want . . .
Coke.'"

His face contorted, he screamed, "CAHN'T SAYEE
THAAHT!" Then abruptly he wheeled and ran off in the
direction of the cottage.

When I next encountered Scott, I reluctantly explained
to him what had happened. The incident seemed disastrous
to me, a major step backward, but Scott again reined me in.

"I wouldn't worry about it. Actually, it's a good sign.
He's really dealing with you, that's the important thing. At
least he told you off, and that's a good indication that you've
gotten a toehold on his psyche. Remember, this is a kid who
hasn't expressed a feeling or said anything to anyone for a
long time. Now he's relating—and that's progress, Pat!"

I wasn't totally convinced that there wouldn't be some
negative carry-over from the incident, but I was determined

to follow my plan to make demands on Mike. It seemed the only thing to do. I let a couple of days slide by so that he could think things over. Then I called his teacher and asked her to tell Mike I'd be up for him after school that afternoon. He was sitting in the dayroom when I arrived, and I gestured toward the open door, then followed him outside.

"It'll be quieter and easier this way to plan what we want to do today, Mike. Now I'd like you to tell me again what you want to do, but say it loud enough so I can hear right away. Okay?"

Mike was looking down, intently studying the tangle of knots that topped off one hiking boot.

"Say it loud now, Mike, and then we'll be off."

He raised his head slightly but did not look at me. "Hike dugfahs," he muttered, quickly glancing down again.

"Good, Mike. I heard you fine that time. And if that's what you want to do, that's what we'll do. We'll hike 'dug-fahs.' That was very, *very* good!" Abruptly, an idea crossed my mind. "Mike, is 'dugfahs' what you call the hill where we hike? Is that a name?"

An all-but-imperceptible nod. Then Mike gazed off in the direction of the bluff. "Dugfahs . . . Dugfahs . . . Dugfahs . . . " he whispered, almost as if it were a force pulling him.

I tried again to understand. "Dugfahs . . . Dugface . . . *Dog*face? Is that your name for the hill—*Dogface?*"

Again, eyes down, the faint nod.

"Well, that's great, Mike; that's a very good name. Let's go hike Dogface."

CHAPTER SIX

THE ROCKY OUTCROPPING THAT ROSE UP BEHIND THE Children's Unit bore no resemblance that I could see to a dog's face or head; the name Mike had given it had apparently emerged out of sheer fantasy. "Dogface" was part of a range of jagged hills, blanketed with rough bushes that scraped your legs as you walked along the narrow animal trails. There were gravelly washes of decomposed rock, and here and there gigantic sets of boulders clung together as if for support against their common enemy, the elements.

Near the top, the terrain became almost inaccessible. The millenia of weather had worked their magic, combining with volcanic nuances to leave a series of deep cuts on the high rock faces. Mike's little spot was a relatively easy climb that circumvented the more difficult heights. But sometimes he had sought out different routes and over the months I came to recognize the challenge and the allure that hiking on Dogface held for him.

Since some verbal communication was being established, I was primed for the next step. Even though Mike still kept his distance, there were times now when he yielded a bit. It had taken over four months, but on occasion I was finally permitted to draw within ten feet or so before he became antsy. I was learning to deal in fractions. Since his consuming interest was in "hiking Dogface," I began to think about how I could increase communication by devising another task that would be within reach and at the same time help to strengthen our relationship.

Seeing some of the other children coloring pictures one day gave me an idea, and the next time I went up to the cottage I took along some drawing paper and crayons. Mike's eyebrows arched slightly when he saw me beckoning him to come into the dayroom, and his eyes narrowed as he spotted the drawing materials next to the chair where he usually sat. He hesitated a few moments, then went to the window and looked out, his back toward me.

"Mike, what would you like to do today?"

"Hike Dugfahs," came back, a flat monotone glazed over with suspicion.

"Good, Mike, that's very good; but first I want you to do one thing—draw a picture. Will you do that? Then we'll be off for Dogface, okay?"

Mike continued to stare out the window, steadfastly ignoring the paper and crayons. I settled in for a marathon session, watching him closely and trying to read something from his expression. It was impossible, though, to tell whether his noncompliance was stubbornness, or whether he was withdrawing again, retreating from me.

For a full half-hour Mike sat in stony silence, never moving except when he blinked. Every so often I would try to goad him, but again it seemed as if a battle of wills were taking place between us.

Another ten minutes elapsed and I was getting fidgety. Maybe I had gone too far again, pushing for too much. But progress had to come sometime; if I didn't press for more, we wouldn't get any further.

Finally I said, "Mike, if you don't draw a picture soon, it's going to be too late for us to hike up Dogface. I have to be back for a meeting and we've got only an hour left. C'mon, draw the picture so we can take off."

No response. If anything, I detected a stiffening of the shoulders—and the resolve. We sat in silence until I felt the point of no return had been reached.

"Okay, Mike, I guess we'll just have to miss our hike to Dogface today. That's too bad; I know it's hard for you, but you think about it—think about drawing that picture for me next time and then we can hike. I'll see you tomorrow, buddy."

Mike didn't move as I unlocked the dayroom door and walked down to the nursing station to tell them we wouldn't be leaving. I talked with the nurse on duty for a few minutes and when I returned to the dayroom, Mike was gone.

The paper and crayons, untouched for over an hour, were now scattered all over the floor. . . .

The next day there was a message for me from Cecile, Mike's teacher. All morning he had been jumping up and down, pacing, and jabbering, and she wondered whether his behavior was a result of something going on in therapy. I showed the note to Scott.

"That's another good sign; maybe not on the surface— usually we're more apt to feel like we're making progress when a child *isn't* disruptive—but Mike's really struggling with some issues, and he may begin to act out like this now and then. Talk with Cecile so she understands what's happening and ask her to let you know whenever Mike does something unusual. You'd better also tell the cottage staff to expect some misbehavior, but not to punish him. Encourage him to work it through."

Right after lunch I met with Cecile and filled her in, then compared notes with the nurses and aides at Mike's cottage. Later, as soon as classes were out, I strolled back up there, crayons and paper tucked under my arm. It was a perfect day for a hike, with lacy cirrus clouds strung delicately across the azure sky. I knew that wouldn't be lost on Mike and I hoped it would provide an impetus for cooperation.

I found him looking a bit sulky, curled up in his regular chair near the window. As I greeted him, I pushed the paper and crayons down the table to him.

"Boy, is it ever *beautiful* out there, Mike! What do you want to do today?"

"Hike Dugfahs."

"Okay, fine. But you know what you have to do first. Did you think about drawing that picture for me? Can you do that today, Mike?

Silence.

"Please give it a try, Mike. Then we'll take off for Dogface."

Several moments passed, then there was a hesitating movement. Finally Mike turned and straightened the paper. His shoulders sagged as he halfheartedly picked up a crayon and scribbled a stick person. Then he stopped to await my verdict.

"Goooooood, Mike!" I was amazed at how well this was working and even caught myself drawing out the "good" as Lovaas had done. "That's great, Mike. Okay, let's be on our way. . . ."

Two days later I was back again. This time Mike went obediently to the table and quickly sketched another stick figure, then dropped his hands to his lap.

"Mike," I said as gently as possible, "that's fine, but I need a little more—you can draw a better picture than that. Please try."

He sighed and picked up the crayon again. Then other crayons. He drew two more stick people, faces blank, and a grid of lines that made them appear to be in jail, behind a dark, forbidding door. Once more he stopped.

"Goooood! That's a fine picture. What is it, Mike? What did you draw?"

"Heah," he mumbled, his voice barely audible.

"Ah, that's your cottage here, where you live?"

A slight nod.

"Okay, Mike, very good. Now what shall we do?"

"Hike Dugfahs *nowww!*" came out emphatically. He was poised on the edge of his chair ready to spring for the door.

"Sure, Mike, that's great! You're really doing fine!"

The picture he had drawn seemed to characterize aptly his perception of the hospital—kids barricaded in, imprisoned by the always-locked door. I couldn't help but wonder what it was like for him, as he took these first steps toward reality.

At our next meeting I laid the crayons and paper down on a table and moved away. Mike glanced at the materials, went to the window for a brief look, then turned and sat down beside them. It was as if he needed to remind himself that what was to come would be worth all this trouble.

"Will you draw another picture for me, Mike, so we can go on our hike?"

Mike contemplated the paper and then he abruptly reached for the crayons. Again the stick figures with no discernible features, standing alongside what I guessed to be a tree.

As he moved away from the picture, I walked over and examined it more closely. "That's very good, Mike, but why don't the people have faces?"

I retreated from the paper and Mike walked back, stared briefly at the page, then swiftly pushed it away.

"Hike Dugfahs NOW!"

"Okay, Mike. You've done everything I've asked of you. You deserve a hike—and maybe a double-decker chocolate ice cream cone, too."

He looked over at me, and for an instant his expression softened at the prospect of a treat. But a second later the spontaneity was gone, and the veil of flatness descended once again.

Yet later that afternoon, as we were returning from Dogface, Mike did something that astonished me. We were approaching the canteen when he suddenly blurted out,

"We geh ah-eese creeemcone!"

I stared at him. Had I heard him right? Did he say *we*?

Hearing Mike talk about doing something with me was perhaps a small step. But then I was learning, as Scott had said, that there would be no miracles, just tiny gains reflected in a word here, a look there.

Later, Scott went over the pictures with me. He was impressed. "This is a good start. A child, and especially one who is disturbed, can tell you so much about his inner dynamics with a drawing. In fact, sometimes you can get information it would be difficult to get any other way. You know, there are some good signs here."

"Where?" The pictures looked pretty bleak to me.

"Well, the first thing is that he drew people, so people are a part of his world. Or are starting to be. He said 'we' today, and that's pretty consistent with what he's done here. I think all your time and work with Mike may be starting to pay off." He paused for a moment. "The blank faces are interesting, aren't they?"

"I asked him about that, but he didn't answer. What do you make of the rest?"

Scott looked thoughtfully at the drawings spread out before him. "Well, we've got some primitive stick people, a rather barren tree, a cottage with everyone locked in. It's about what we might expect from someone with Mike's background. The darkened tones would perhaps indicate some depression, but that'd be understandable, too. Mike hasn't had much to be happy about."

"Yeh."

"Did you ask Mike if he's in either of these pictures?"

"No. Should I?"

Scott nodded. "Try asking him. See if you can get some

descriptions. Start working him toward telling you stories about what he draws. It might be very revealing."

"Okay."

"Then begin dating these and keep them in order. They may come in handy and be even more helpful as therapy progresses. I'd have him draw on a regular basis. Encourage him to use colors, open himself up to the world. Mike's beginning to use you as the go-between to a world he's never known, but you're going to have to be the one to lead the way."

CHAPTER SEVEN

IT WAS MORE OF AN IMPULSE THAN ANYTHING ELSE. I HAD attended a weekend workshop in Santa Cruz and, while planning my route back to Merrick, I saw the name Reidsville. I remembered that that was where Mike's parents lived. Since I hadn't been able to reach them any other way, why not drop in? Maybe I could find out why they had never answered any of my letters, and perhaps even learn something about Mike's early years. Besides, I was curious.

Fortunately, Reidsville turned out to be quite small. I stopped at an old service station to ask where the Harrises lived. The teenager who filled my tank told me and added, with a smirk, "You can't miss the shrine."

He was right. In the front yard, standing on its partially buried end, was an enormous old white enamel bathtub. This bit of recycling wizardry served as a shelter for a child-sized statue of the Virgin Mary. Plaster-of-Paris sheep lay at her feet and a half circle of small whitewashed stones and bright plastic flowers completed the tableau.

The house was a rambling one with an air of perpetual

renovation. It had several additions, all of which seemed to have been built with whatever was available at the time. Two different shades of blue aluminum siding overlay one wall, a patch of redwood ran up to some exposed tar paper on another, and even the roof sections were two colors of shingle. Bricks, lumber, and odd lengths of aluminum siding lay here and there. Mr. Harris was evidently an accomplished scrounger.

At the end of the driveway stood a rusty Cadillac Fleetwood that I guessed to be ten or eleven years old. Its massive hood was open, a small figure draped over the fender as if in the process of being swallowed by a gigantic lizard.

"Mr. Harris?"

I approached the car and peered into the cavernous inner workings.

"Yeh." Irritated at being interrupted, he blinked at me through the sweat and grease that had seeped into his eyes. He buried his head in a sleeve for a moment, then gave me a sharp look. "You better not be selling something on a Sunday—"

"No, no. I'm Patrick McGarry, Mike's therapist at the state hospital."

"Oh . . . " Mr. Harris's head descended back into the engine.

"I was up at a meeting in Santa Cruz and thought I'd stop by and see you and your wife, let you know how Mike is doing. Is Mrs. Harris here?"

"Yeh, but she's not feeling too well today. And stuff about Mike upsets her."

"I see. Well, do you suppose it would be too much of a strain on her to hear about Mike? Actually, he's been doing fairly well lately."

Mr. Harris was very intent on tightening something. His face twisted as he bore down on the ratchet, then unexpectedly the bolt broke and his hand plunged against the radiator. Leaping back, he cursed, slammed down the hood, and turned on me. "You coulda just sent a letter, you know. You didn't have to come all the way out here and bother us."

So Mike's progress was a "bother" to them . . . "I've never been too sure my letters have gotten to you. Besides, I thought you might like to know about Mike firsthand."

Mr. Harris grunted; his eyes narrowed as he studied me. "Whyd' ya hide your face behind a beard? Only hippies and commies wear beards."

I just shrugged and smiled. Mr. Harris's jowly jaw looked as if it had been shaved with a straight razor. I remembered from the case history that he was only a year or two older than I, but he seemed already middle-aged, worn down, his slack shoulders gravitating toward a small paunch.

Abruptly he swung toward the side door of the house. "Wait here," he said. After a few minutes he returned. "Don't talk too much in there now. My wife gets upset very easy. She's not a strong woman."

I followed Mr. Harris through the kitchen and into the living room. The furnishings were shabby but everything was clean and neat, a noticeable contrast from the mess outside. I guessed that Mrs. Harris took care of the interior, but then I wondered if she was capable. Although the hospital record had painted a dismal picture of Mike's mother, I was still startled by the emaciated woman who sat cowering in a rocker, a Bible clutched in her hands. When she saw me, she cringed.

"You're . . . you're not going to take me back to the hospital, are you?" Her fingers began making little fluttering movements as they ran up and down the edges of the Bible.

"No, Mrs. Harris. I'm Patrick McGarry. I'm from the Children's Unit at—"

"There's no need to worry, Mother," Mr. Harris interceded. "He's not from *that* hospital. He's from Merrick, where Mikey is. No need to get upset now." He moved near her and put his hand protectively on her shoulder.

Mrs. Harris relaxed somewhat, but her expression now was one of bewilderment. "Mike?" she asked, as if the name were new to her. "Mike?" she repeated. She raised her eyes beseechingly toward her husband.

"That's okay, dear," he responded and then glanced uneasily at me. "My wife has spells. She's a little confused today."

Suddenly recognition flooded her face. "Oh yes, *Michael*. Michael, the Archangel . . . " She smiled sweetly at me, as if pleased to make the connection.

What the hell was going on here? "No, Mrs. Harris, Michael your son. He's almost nine years old now, goes to school, and loves to hike in the hills behind the hospital . . . " My voice trailed off as I realized that she wasn't listening. She was mumbling under her breath, forming silent words and twisting a handkerchief back and forth in her hands. Her face had a familiar vacant look. I remembered the social worker's observation that Mrs. Harris was probably a borderline psychotic. No longer borderline, I amended to myself.

Abruptly Mr. Harris leaned over, plucked the Bible from his wife's lap, and began waving it in front of me. He was suddenly flooded with energy. "We've always known what was wrong with our Mikey. I don't know why you people can't see it! It was Satan who got hold of him. Demons possessed him just like the Bible says—it was God's punishment for our sins, our misdeeds. Somewhere along the way we broke God's Law and, in His Almighty Wisdom, He saw fit to punish us through Mikey. The Power of God demonstrated once again!"

I kept looking at Mrs. Harris, whose fingers were now wearing a groove in the arm of her chair. She had hunched over as though lashed by her husband's words and I thought she was crying.

". . . the Power of Prayer," Mr. Harris thundered on. "Let us bow our heads in prayer!"

I looked at him questioningly. What had I gotten into?

"Bow your head!" he demanded. "We're going to pray for salvation." He glared at me until I complied. "Our God in Heaven . . . " he intoned, Bible held high in the air.

I kept my head down, staring at the pattern in the worn rug until it began to swirl. Occasionally I peeked at Mrs. Harris, who now had her hands clasped in fervent prayer. A look of beatific bliss played across her face. Mr. Harris prayed for twenty minutes straight and I was rocking on my heels by the time he wound down to a hoarse, "Amen." I mumbled a heartfelt one myself.

Mrs. Harris raised her arms longingly toward heaven and I noted a remarkable resemblance between her and Mike; it was not so much a matter of features as of the same reflexive flinch that I had seen so often in her son, an alertness and guardedness as though she expected momentarily to be struck. As she gazed at the ceiling, I could tell from her varying expressions that she was in some kind of religious ecstasy, or maybe hallucinating. Then her eyes settled back down on me and she smiled benignly. We regarded each other for a few moments and I felt genuinely moved. She was a gentle as well as frightened creature and I could readily understand why her husband was so protective of her. I recognized, too, that she was once again in contact with reality, so I pressed on with my message.

"I just wanted you both to know that Mike is fine. He and I spend a lot of time together hiking in the hills behind Merrick. Mike's gotten to be quite a little mountain climber. And he's growing like a weed—you wouldn't recognize him . . . " My voice faded as I realized the import of my words.

But Mr. Harris didn't notice. "Does Mike still have those spells? Those awful screaming fits?"

"Not really. But then he doesn't come near people yet, either. As long as he isn't pushed, and we don't expect too much of him for the time being, he's pretty quiet and cooperative. He's talking a little now, and is learning to ask for things. He likes chocolate ice cream cones—"

I broke off as Mrs. Harris's head slowly sank and the mumbling resumed. She seemed to be losing her fragile hold again. I looked questioningly at Mr. Harris and he pointed toward the door. Nodding, I bent over and said, "I have to be going now, Mrs. Harris. It was nice meeting you . . . "

The trance persisted and I straightened to find Mr. Harris beside me. We both tiptoed quietly from the room. When we reached the driveway, he paused and asked, "Do you believe in the Power of Prayer?" His manner was almost friendly now. My participation in the marathon prayer had apparently mollified him.

"Well, yes, sort of . . . " I hedged. Then I summoned up my courage. "I'd like to ask you to do something, Mr. Harris."

"What's that?"

"Get some professional help for your wife. Take her to the community mental health center. For her sake, and yours, too. I know she'll probably be frightened, but just tell them that before you take her in and they'll understand. Perhaps they can prescribe something so she doesn't have so many spells, as you call them. It's terrible for her to be in such a state, Mr. Harris. Something could happen to her while you're at work. And that could be avoided. There are things that can be done."

"She gets along okay."

All I could do was shake my head. He still didn't recognize how disturbed she was, any more than he had appreciated a few years ago how imperative it was for Mike to get into therapy. "Mr. Harris." He looked up at me and our eyes met. "She needs professional help. Please get her some."

"Well, Mr. McGarry, I suppose you mean well. But I reckon we'll just stick with our own ways. We get along okay."

"What about your son, Mr. Harris?"

"Our minister has told us to stay away from him, because of the demon possession. He says Michael is no longer ours, that he's been taken over—"

"Well, he *is* yours," I interrupted. "Mike is still your child even though he's seriously disturbed. He's a very sensitive kid, Mr. Harris, and you shouldn't just write him off."

He dropped his eyes. "What're his chances?"

"I honestly can't tell you. I'm trying to help him, but I just can't say how far he'll be able to come. No one at Merrick can. But we do know we need your help. You can contribute, especially if Mike continues to make progress."

"You know, I never thought there was much anyone

could do; leastways that's what the minister says. I dunno. Could I maybe come out and see him sometime?"

Boy, I thought, I'd sure like to square off with that minister. "Of course, Mr. Harris. But first I'd want you to take your wife to the mental health center and get that help for her. She really needs it. I should think it would take a big load off you if she were in a better frame of mind."

We shook hands and though I never expected to see or hear from him again—nor was I hopeful that he would go to the mental health center—I was glad I had stopped in. At least I had tried . . .

Dismaying as my experience with the Harrises was, its net effect was to help me see—and perhaps more important, feel—Mike's problems in the context of that devastated family. My visit had given Mike a history. He was no longer just the little bundle of symptoms and fears and resistances I was trying to counteract, of potential resources I was attempting to mobilize. He now loomed in my mind as a child with a past, like any other. The child of that fanatical father and woebegone mother. And if I didn't understand his plight any better, I certainly felt it more keenly and toughened my resolve to do whatever I could for him. But I was concerned about something else—only six months remained in my internship, and I wondered just how much I could accomplish in that period.

Mike turned nine early in December, but when I tried to explain what his birthday meant, he simply looked blank. However, he didn't have any trouble understanding the hot fudge sundae I treated him to at the canteen.

Two weeks after his birthday, Mike was wandering among the cottage Christmas decorations. But if he sensed any difference at all from the rest of the year, it didn't show.

CHAPTER EIGHT

JANUARY AND FEBRUARY WERE UNSEASONABLY COLD AND rainy and, more often than not, we postponed our hikes. From his post by the dayroom window, Mike kept a close eye on the elements. Sometimes I'd prop the door open, but he would refuse to leave. On other occasions, he might venture out but would then abruptly turn around and lope back to the cottage, having seemingly had his fill of the blustery weather.

With the arrival of better hiking conditions, I decided the first order of business should be to get Mike to come physically closer to me. I had tried various ways of coaxing him to do so, but although he had reduced the distance somewhat, he consistently maintained the boundaries of his space. I had rarely been able to penetrate them—and then only for seconds.

I knew that this was pretty much an approximation of the psychological distance that Mike wanted to preserve. It was his way of protecting himself; he was still far from being able to take chances with me or anyone else. But this meant, in effect, that we had reached an impasse: Mike listened to me and did what I suggested if he were so inclined, but otherwise I remained simply an observer of his solitary activities.

It was apparent, then, that I had to think of a new tactic if I were to set things in motion again. One afternoon shortly after Mike and I had left the lemon grove, some vivid pictures from a magazine article I had recently read popped into my mind. The photographs showed two mountain climbers scaling a steep summit, and the text had stressed the importance of their teamwork.

Well, it was worth a try. I had done some climbing in the past and figured we could handle some of the ridges without too much danger. Ahead of me was a rock wall that Mike, trotting along up the path, had already passed. I called out to him, "Mike, let's try going up this way; we can get to the top quicker."

I scrambled up the draw, using the mesquite bushes as handholds. Then, when I reached the wall, I began creeping slowly up a narrow fissure in the granite face. Halfway up I paused, out of breath, and looked down at Mike, who was standing on the trail, intently watching me.

"Hey, this is fun," I yelled. "It's like mountain climbing. C'mon." I twisted along, inched through some loose shale and, pulling myself onto a ledge, I stood up. From here Mike was just a small figure.

"C'mon, Mike. This is great," I shouted. "But watch your footing—it's steep!"

Mike was gazing up at me and I wondered whether he'd follow. But then he began clambering through the brush to the wall. I coached him to place his feet carefully and to test the footing before shifting his weight. Within a short time he was just below me. As he neared the ledge, I knelt down and extended my hand.

"Here, Mike, let me help you." Then I added, "Hikers have to work together!"

Ignoring the outstretched hand, Mike circled around me. But I sensed a possibility—he had seemed intrigued as he picked his way up the wall. After that I began to search for more difficult and rugged terrain that was still reasonably safe. It seemed to be an adventure for Mike, because each time he would come immediately to the spot I had selected and then, after watching me ascend, he would follow. I noticed, too, that he often traced my steps and planted his feet as he had seen me do.

Mike was listening and learning, so I continued to offer climbing advice and encouragement and, although his expression remained distant and noncommittal, it was clear that he was eager to climb. I always went first so that at difficult spots or at resting points I would be waiting, my hand extended for a helping boost. As he'd get close, I'd say, "C'mon, Mike. Take my hand. It's okay—remember, hikers have to work together."

But he would have none of it, and after a few weeks of scaling various routes, I began to get discouraged again. There had not been the slightest inkling that Mike might accept my idea of working together; even on a narrow rock shelf, he managed to maintain as much psychological distance as before. Also, as Mike's prowess increased and we attempted more challenging climbs, I became concerned about the hazards. What if Mike fell? I had a professional as well as a personal responsibility for him. I had discussed this with Scott after the first climb and he had concurred that the possibility of real gain was worth the small risk. But with the risk increasing and no gain in sight, I was on the verge of giving up.

"Besides," I told Scott, "if reaching out hasn't worked yet, it's probably not going to. We should have seen something, some reaction, by now. I think it's just too big a jump for him."

Scott didn't reply immediately; then a slow smile crept across his face and he chuckled. "You know, I'd really like to see you guys up there sometime. I have this mental image of you swinging out on a cliff, dangling from a rock by one hand, and yelling, 'C'mon, Mike, hikers have to work togetherrrrrrrrr!'"

I smiled, but I didn't think it was very funny.

"Seriously, Pat," he went on, "we know how much Mike loves to get up in the hills and now there's his new interest in climbing. Sooner or later he may just understand the importance of teamwork. Why don't you try it a few more times? After all, what else have you got?"

One day two weeks later Mike and I were on the march again. With over eight months of tramping the hills behind us, we were nearing the summit of Dogface from the back —the south side—which was much more precipitous than our usual routes. We had stopped many times before to scout the mottled rock wall, but had always gone on. It just seemed too difficult and dangerous to attempt. By now, though, Mike had become a surefooted and nimble little climber, and as we passed a gap he threw an appraising glance up the wall. So I challenged him.

"Shall we go for the top from this side, Mike?" I nodded toward the cliff. "I don't know. . . . It'll be a tough climb —think we can do it?"

He stopped and looked back at me, then up the ridge. After several moments of hesitation, he started back toward me and I took the opportunity to remind him, "Now Mike, this is the kind of climbing where hikers have to work together, help each other out. It's going to be hard. So if you need any help, sing out! Agreed?"

This time I really meant it, but he remained impassive, eyes riveted upon the ridge.

I began to climb. The first dozen yards to the wall were relatively easy going, but then as I hit a patch of gravel on rock, I was scrambling on all fours in an effort to make headway up the steep incline. Farther up, some roots protruding from the bank offered a temporary respite. While I rested I scanned the next stretch and then, planning the route to take from there, I noted where the granite seemed decomposed and likely to be brittle.

Mike stood motionless at the bottom, watching me.

"Well, this is it," I said under my breath, and pushed off from the bank. Swinging across the gully, I used my momentum to reach a narrow ledge, pressing hard against the cold rock face while I searched for safe handholds. When I'd found some, I began to climb again, selecting and testing my holds, then shifting my weight carefully, kicking away loose rocks. A little farther on I stopped again to assess my route and position, and to give Mike a progress report over my shoulder.

"This seems to be a pretty good way, Mike. But watch the loose rock and be sure to get good handholds. Dig those boots in!"

Mike remained motionless, observing me intently.

But the next part was harder than I had anticipated and by the time I was halfway up the wall my arms were aching.

Finally, after another ten minutes, I pulled myself into a large crevice in the rocks just below the crest of the ridge. Panting and gasping, I sagged against the opening. As soon as I caught my breath, I yelled down:

"Mike, forget it! It's too dangerous! Go around the other way and I'll meet you at the top. I'm going to rest here for a few minutes."

But I was too late. After making sure that I was not going to dislodge any more rocks, Mike had already started after me and the loose shale clattering behind him drowned out my warning. All I could do was watch—and feel a growing concern. Maybe this time I *had* gone too far.

Mike traversed the bottom quickly and soon reached the steeper part. Now that he could hear me again, I repeated my earlier warning, urging him to go around the other way. But to no avail. He was bent on scaling that wall and there was nothing I could do to stop him. I could only watch as he crisscrossed the ridge, studying the route and wending his way along the ledges and cracks. When he was about halfway up, he disappeared behind a shelf that jutted out at an angle away from the cliff wall. Then there was silence; perhaps he had stopped to catch his wind.

"That's right. Take a rest, Mike," I counseled.

A few moments later the sound of dropping rock indicated he was moving again and then his head came into view some twenty feet below me. He was sweating and his face was streaked with dirt. I could see that he was scared.

I moved down near the edge and braced myself.

"Just a little bit farther, Mike. Carefully now—you can make it okay."

Pulling himself up hand over hand, he was concentrating hard on not looking down. He still looked frightened, but a strong sense of achievement seemed to be propelling him on. His expression was determined. For the last few yards between us the going was treacherous, the rock broken and slippery, and as he came across this last stretch I reached out toward him, extending my hand as before.

"Here, Mike, let me help you."

At precisely that moment his footing gave way and he began to slip sideways. In that split second pure instinct took over and, lurching forward, he grasped my hand. I pulled hard, practically yanking him off his feet and into the narrow gap where I had been waiting. Adrenaline pumping, we collapsed together against the cliff—not a foot apart.

It wasn't the way I would have chosen to have it happen. He had slipped, and grabbed more out of desperation than anything else. But I was willing to take whatever I could get.

"Mike, you did some great climbing there—you're getting to be a real pro!"

He sat trembling beside me, arms clasped tightly around his knees, exhausted by the strain and fright of the climb. I could almost hear his little heart drumming away; it had been too close a call for him.

I reached over and rested my hand gently on his shoulder. "Hikers really do have to work together, don't they, Mike?" Then I took a moment to point out the importance of what had just happened—how much we both needed each other, depended on each other for help and support.

Mike was too wrung out to protest my touching him, much less move away. He just huddled there, still shaken by the exertion and shock. During the twenty minutes or so that we rested on that rock ledge I was physically closer to him than I had ever been. I felt good about that. Even though I knew he was just too spent to budge, I was thinking that what had happened once could more easily happen again. Gradually the color returned to Mike's face and he seemed to be recovering. Time to move on.

"Last one to the top's a monkey's uncle!" I challenged.

Mike gave me a quizzical look. Then, haltingly, he said, "Munng-key uhnn-koe?"

The little freckled face, all squinched up in an effort to understand, made me burst out laughing. For the first time, it was Mike who was puzzled—and showing it—and trying to comprehend something I had said.

"That's just a saying, Mike," I explained. "A monkey's uncle is just a funny expression. C'mon, you ready to go for the top?" I motioned toward the summit and Mike got up, still looking slightly perplexed, and began to climb up out of the gap.

Later on that afternoon as we bushwhacked down through a steep talus field, I offered Mike my hand again, but he went on by. As I watched his heel-digging descent, I wondered fleetingly whether we would ever be as close as we had been earlier. In any event, I knew it was absolutely essential that I follow up on what had happened on the south face.

"Mike, shall we hike up Dogface again tomorrow?"

From twenty feet away his reply came quickly, without hesitation, "Hike up Dugfahs tumawah!"

"Okay, and I hope you'll let me help you again. Hikers really do have to take care of each other."

I sensed he was studying me and I glanced at him; but when our eyes met, he quickly looked away.

Mike was still drawing pictures before our hikes, and after grabbing my hand I hoped the experience would be represented in his next drawing. It wasn't. Taking the crayons, he painstakingly drew a house and a stick figure. He had drawn this same picture dozens of times, occasionally with different colors or with more figures. But the people were always the same, and always without faces.

So I didn't know what kind of impact our dangerous climb had had until we were on Dogface again the next day.

After leaving the crayons and drawing at the nursing station, we headed for the hole in the fence, slid through, and
tramped along in silence. I had in mind a particular escarp-
ment that I thought would offer a safer climbing challenge.
When I stopped, Mike also halted not far behind me, and
I pointed toward the craglike ridge that rose before us.

"This is one we haven't climbed yet, Mike. Want to
give it a try?" Without waiting for an answer I started forward, knowing that Mike would not be inclined to refuse.
About halfway up, a ledge widened considerably and there,
where powerful volcanic forces had heaved the wall, I could
spot where the ledge reversed itself and changed direction.
It was a somewhat tricky climb, and when I pulled myself
onto the shelf, I realized it was the perfect setup.

"Mike, I'm going to stop here," I shouted down. "Why
don't you come on up?"

He didn't have to be asked a second time. Rapidly he
wound his way to the base and began the ascent. After five
minutes of hard climbing, he ducked into a granite cleft not
far below me.

"Take a breather, Mike. This next part is harder, so
rest. And remember, hikers have to work together, so if you
need a hand, say so and let me help you. Sometime I may
need some help myself, and I'll certainly ask for it if I do,
okay?"

Without giving any evidence of having heard me, Mike
resumed the climb. He was careful yet sure in his movements
and in a few moments was standing just below my position
on the ledge.

Reaching out toward him, I said, "Here, Mike, take
my hand. I'll help you up."

He squinted at my outstretched hand, studying it as if
there might be an extra finger. Then he gazed across the

cliffside and down, apparently retracing the course he had just scaled. He was clearly caught in a conflict, his darting eyes betraying uncertainty and anxiety. And then, as if remembering what had happened the previous day, he extended his arm to where I could just grab his hand. I drew him up the last few feet and he sank onto the terrace beside me.

"Great, Mike! That's the way—that's how hikers work together!"

We sat together in silence for a few minutes and then I pointed out a small lizard that had popped out from behind a rock to inspect the company. We watched it for a while, sprawled side by side against the rock, and Mike didn't seem to mind the closeness.

After a time I said, "Okay, Mike, ready for the top?"

His reply was immediate and emphatic.

"Hike top Dugfahs!"

I looked sharply at him. Edging into the monotone I was so used to, his voice carried the hint of excitement. A subtle inflection I couldn't be sure of, and yet . . .

We moved off the ledge and the surprises continued. Instead of reverting to his usual distance, Mike stayed close to me and, side by side, we climbed to the top of Dogface. I couldn't recall a time when I had felt more encouraged and rewarded as we sat beside each other on the crest. It had taken such a long time, but at last Mike was allowing me inside his magic circle.

Forty-five minutes later as we approached the cottage door, Mike was still walking near me. As I took out my keys to let him in, I said, "Mike, I want you to know how very proud of you I am, and how happy I am that you gave me your hand so I could help you. I know it was hard for you, and that makes it a very brave thing that you did. Sometimes it's scary to take a chance and trust someone, but I'm glad you were able to do it again today, and I hope you'll do it some more. And Mike . . . " by this time he was shifting his weight impatiently from one foot to the other, "I also want you to know that it's just super to have my hiking buddy as close to me as you have been this afternoon. That feels very, very good to me, and I hope it does to you, too. You're really a good friend, and it's nice to do things together."

Mike was staring intently at the door. But when I opened it, he gave me one quick glance and our eyes met momentarily before he slid out of view. But that was enough. He had heard and understood what I said. I was sure of it.

During the following week, Mike alternated between coming near me and shying away, as if uncertain from moment to moment what his attitude should be. For my part, I didn't push it. Except for one occasion.

We were hiking down from the summit, playing a game I had taught Mike of jumping from rock to rock. When we cleared the boulderfield, I noticed that he was limping slightly. Catching up with him, I saw that he was holding his hand on the inside of his upper thigh, and walking fast, rather stiff-legged. When he saw my concerned look, he began hobbling even faster.

"Mike, what's wrong? Did you hurt yourself back there?"

He shook his head and stepped up his pace.

As I stood there watching him shuffle along, a memory circuit clicked. I had seen a gait like that before. And then it hit me: when we took the blind children on field trips, the rest rooms were always unfamiliar. Some of the kids, not wanting to contend with strange toilets, would try to hold back too long. As parents do, I quickly learned to anticipate such problems; it was always easy to spot a child in that distress. That's how Mike looked now, as though he was literally trying to hold it in. Suddenly it occurred to me that on all our hikes I had never seen him relieve himself. On a couple of occasions I had stepped behind some rocks, and I had assumed Mike did the same.

"Mike, do you have to go to the toilet?"

No reaction.

"Mike, if you have to pee, just walk over behind those rocks. You don't have to wait till we get all the way back to the cottage. Is that what you're trying to do? Mike?"

He slowed, and then stopped. He wouldn't turn to face me so I went around in front of him. Sure enough, he was holding his hand in the inimitable manner of small children when they *really* have to go.

"Mike, just go on over to those big rocks there. It's okay to pee."

He shook his head, still looking down.

"Why not? Why won't you?"

"Bahd."

"It's not bad, Mike. Who ever told you that?"

"Bahd," he repeated.

"No, it's not; it's a very natural thing. Peeing, going to the bathroom, is okay—just like eating and drinking. What goes in must come out!" I said it lightly, but Mike didn't make the connection. "It's okay for you to go out here, Mike. That's what people do when they camp, or when they go hiking and there's no toilet around."

He still wasn't moving, other than squirming from foot to foot. And then I thought, What the hell, I sort of have to go too. I'll set an example.

"C'mon, Mike, I'll join you. Let's go over there."

Sensing that Mike was shy, I added, "You take one side of that big rock and I'll take the other. C'mon, I don't like to see you hurting like this."

I wheeled in the direction of the large boulders at the base of the cliff and he reluctantly followed.

"You'll feel a heck of a lot better," I said, unzipping my fly.

Mike looked furtively around, then at me for one last signal of reassurance, and hastily opened his pants. Within seconds, the relief on his face was so evident I laughed.

"See, doesn't that feel a lot better?"

"Fews gooooood!"

"Right, I told you it would. There's no point in suffering like that, is there? From now on, whenever you're hiking and you have to go, just find a nice rock or a tree. There's nothing 'bad' about it."

Little of consequence happened with Mike over the next month. But in other ways, things brightened up a bit when Debbie Shaw, a clinical psychologist, joined the staff. Somewhere in her late twenties, she was extremely attractive, a healthy tan softening her distinctive features. She had deep brown eyes that followed your every word and a quick, sunny smile. I eagerly volunteered to show her around and Scott agreed, but then cautioned, "Don't come on too strong with the McGarry charm—she's going through a pretty rough divorce." Nevertheless, Deb and I hit it off immediately, and the kids really took to her, too.

It wasn't long, though, before I began getting impatient again. Mike continued to let me stay closer to him, taking my hand now and then when I manufactured a situation. But that was about it. Occasionally we exchanged comments; but generally he drew his pictures, then we hiked silently to the summit of Dogface, rested, and returned. Something more was called for. So one day, instead of letting him choose the drawing topic, I instructed him:

"Mike, I want you to draw a picture of us hiking on Dogface. Will you do that for me? He sat pensively and I wondered whether his uncertainty reflected an inability to draw a mountain. So I sketched a quick profile and handed it to him. "That's how a mountain looks. Kind of. Now you draw one, but don't forget us. Show Mike and Pat hiking, okay?"

He set to work then and the results were gratifying. It seemed as if he needed just a bit more structure at times. A little nudge now and then.

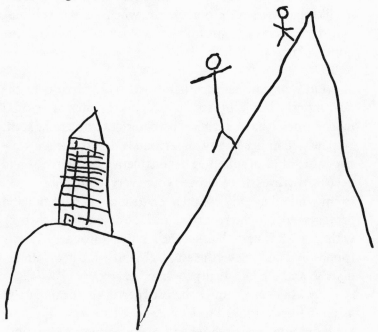

"That's a very good picture, Mike. Very good! Now, can you tell me a story about it?"

Puzzled, Mike stared at what he had drawn.

"Hike Dugfahs."

"Okay, Mike, but first, isn't there anything you can tell me about your picture? I see there are two people. Who are they? Is one of them you?"

A slight nod.

"Can you show me which one is you?"

Slowly, Mike moved his finger and placed it on the smaller figure.

"Good, Mike! Now, am I there, too? Where is Pat?"

The finger slid over a couple of inches and came to rest on the slightly larger form.

"Very, very good, Mike. That's excellent! What are we doing there?"

"Hikin' Dugfahs."

"That's right, we are, aren't we? And what's this?" I pointed to the house.

Mike shrugged. "Cahge . . . "

"Cottage? Your cottage here?"

A single nod. "Hike Dugfahs."

"Okay, Mike, very good. But one more question." I paused. "Why don't Mike and Pat have faces? Why don't we have eyes . . . and noses . . . and mouths?"

Mike turned away, staring out the window, where his refuge awaited. "Hike . . . "

I sighed. "Okay, Mike, you've done very well today. Let's go."

Two weeks later, Mike and I were advancing to the final approach to the crest of Dogface. I had suggested that we again climb the difficult rock face on the south side where Mike had slipped and almost fallen. We hadn't been back to that area since that day, but now Mike unhesitatingly agreed to give it another try. The rock formation was heavily pitted with cracks and, once again, the going was slow as we climbed, one of us on either side of a vertical rift. We went at a much slower pace than the first time, conserving ourselves, and whenever we stopped for a breather, I would tell him:

"Don't forget, Mike, hikers have to work together. So if you need help, let me know."

From time to time one of us would dislodge a rock and then both of us would stop, listening as it clattered and ricocheted to the bottom. It was a reminder that the rock could have been one of us. Then, more carefully, we'd begin climbing again.

Farther up I dropped back, intentionally allowing Mike to gain a lead, and as we neared the summit glimpses of the familiar crest stood out against the cirrus-clouded sky. High overhead a hawk drifted soundlessly, sliding from side to side on the warm air currents. Mike had just cleared the last ridge and without a backward glance was starting up the trail when I found the spot I'd been searching for. In a crevice shadowed by an immense overhang, I braced myself and called out sharply, "Mike! I need some help here—could you come back?"

In a few moments he returned. Kneeling, he peered down into the space where I was lodged.

"I got myself jammed in here somehow," I told him. "Take my hand, get a good grip, and pull hard, okay?" I reached up toward him.

Mike didn't respond immediately. Instead he knelt there, looking at me and at my outstretched hand. Then his head lifted and he gazed out above me, his eyes following the waves of rolling hills, the valleys with their ribbons of orchards melting into the haze, and the silvery ocean beyond. Again there was that lost look—the expression that I had begun to see more and more—an imprint of the confusion that was going on inside him.

Fortunately, I had placed myself in a fairly secure position, because Mike thought long and hard about what he should do. And, as always, all I could do was wait. As he looked back down at me again, I could see the turmoil of his decision, the misgivings mirrored in his eyes. And then, abruptly, he leaned out and reached down a trembling hand, which I quickly grasped tightly.

For once I dispensed with my "hikers" reinforcer—no words were needed this time.

As soon as I had clambered over the edge, Mike immediately stood up and resumed the short walk to the top, where he sought out his favorite rock. I hung back a while, sensing that he might need some time alone. At last I traced his steps and went over to sit beside him, putting my arm gently across his shoulder.

"Thanks for your help, Mike," I said softly. "That's what it's all about—hikers, people—working together."

I squeezed the back of his neck affectionately. Mike had seen me do this to other kids many times and they always squealed with delight when I did it. But for Mike it was different. He was like a young, wild colt, and I patted him reassuringly when I felt a couple of nervous shivers through his thin shirt. That seemed to calm him and we sat together, faces turned toward the warming sun, relaxing in the lingering breezes that meandered over the crest of Dogface.

I found myself thinking back to our first time up here. And how very much had happened . . .

CHAPTER NINE

AFTER THOSE EXTRAORDINARY DAYS ON THE SUMMIT OF Dogface when Mike let me help him and then reached out and assisted me, some undeniable changes began to occur. Slowly the little boy—the child who had been imprisoned inside himself for so long—started to emerge. The transformation was quite subtle initially, reflected in a comment or request, a glance or expression. By now I was sensitized to the nuances, rare as they were. As in climbing the rock faces, each step toward trust was one of weighing the risk, testing the footing carefully, then stepping out—usually forward, but at times halting and backtracking. Still, once Mike made the commitment, as scary as it was for him, he persevered, just as he had on the south wall of Dogface.

The rest of that month was uneventful. Then one afternoon we were sitting in the dayroom, where I had just watched Mike complete a crayon drawing of his favorite theme: the cottage with two figures that represented us. The faces remained blank as usual; even Dogface had not been outlined.

For the two-hundredth time I inspected the scene and then turned to him.

"Okay, Mike, that's a fine picture, but before we take off for Dogface I want you to tell me why the people don't have faces. Why don't you ever draw any faces?" This time I was determined to get an answer.

Mike sat cross-legged, staring somberly at the paper.

"Do you want me to help you? Should I guess why there are no faces?"

Mike shook his head. He was studying the drawing, then he pushed it toward me and stole a quick glance at me before averting his eyes. I couldn't read anything from his expression, but his shoulders hunched slightly as he gazed solemnly at the floor. Sensing a certain thoughtfulness, I pressed as gently as possible, my voice lowered, trying to convey the concern I felt:

"Mike, I know it's hard, but is there a reason for not drawing faces? I'd really like to know—could you share it with me? Please?"

His lips moved, as if he were talking under his breath. "Please, Mike . . . "

The voice that finally emerged was low, husky, the words tumbling out rapidly and strung together.

"Dey-aw-wuk-kin-uduh-way."

"Mike, I couldn't understand you—could you say it a little slower, please?"

A long, almost exasperated sigh.

"Dey aw wuk-kin uduh waaay."

"They're all looking the other way? Is *that* it, Mike—*all the people are looking the other way?!*"

A quick nod.

So that was it, the answer to the riddle of no faces. Ignored and rejected early in his life, Mike believed that everyone was, literally, looking the other way. He saw no faces; just the backs of people's heads.

I whistled a big sigh and Mike looked up at me, startled.

"Mike, what you've just told me really blows me away. . . . Now I understand better—much better—what things must be like for you. But I hope we can change all that for you, Mike, so you can be a happier person. One thing you can be sure of is that I'm not going to be like that. I'm not ever going to look the other way. Hikers—and best friends —have to help each other out, care for each other. And that's what we are, aren't we, Mike? We're best friends, right?"

While I was talking Mike had looked away again, but now his eyes searched my face.

"Munng-key uhnn-koe . . . "

"What? Monkey's uncle? Oh, boy."

Mike seemed to have latched on to that expression. I wasn't sure why. Maybe he just liked the sound of it, the catchy rhythm of the words. Or perhaps that was now his name for me. In any case, with Mike's incredible disclosure, we had rounded another significant corner.

I caught Scott later that same afternoon just as he was heading for the parking lot. "Got time for a bombshell?" I asked.

He set his briefcase down on the walk. "What's up?"

Showing him the picture, I related what had happened earlier.

"They're all looking the other way, huh?" Scott shook his head, studying the drawing thoughtfully. "That's really classic, Pat. The beautiful transparency of the young coming through, completely without guile. Once you reach a child and he begins to relate to you, to trust you, things do have a way of falling nicely into place."

"Still a long way to go."

"Oh sure. But you seem to have found the right key with Mike—it fits and it's opening doors. Now it's just a matter of time and seeing how far the little guy can go. You're starting to uncap some of that straight-arrow honesty that comes with trust, and as long as he begins to identify with you, and introject you—"

"He is, isn't he?"

"Sure he is. Mike is giving up the aloofness, the withdrawal. He's trying reality on for size—throwing in with you, in a psychological sense. Mike will be using you as a conduit in coming to terms with people and how he's going to get along with them."

"What happens next?"

"It's hard to know for sure. Mike may initiate the next step, but it's more likely that you'll have to do it again. Or he might go back and forth about it. We may want to try play therapy one of these days. But for now, trust your own intuition; you'll probably sense how much he can handle before you see it." Scott inspected the drawing again before handing it back to me. "They're all looking the other way. . . . Boy, it's tough to see that kind of stuff in kids." Scott's voice trailed off. After a moment he added, "You know, I think this little guy's going to make it."

"Of course he is, Scott! You had doubts?"

Scott fixed me with a baleful eye. "See you tomorrow, Pat."

Shortly after that I brought up with Scott the subject of my internship. It would be over in a couple of months and I was concerned about Mike. Scott cut me off in midsentence.

"I just assumed you'd stay on and collect the data for your dissertation right here. No need to move on to do that. Here are the papers and stuff I need you to sign, though, if you decide to stick around and take a staff position. It'll pay a little better, too . . . " He pushed the forms at me. They'd already been made out, except for my signature.

For once, I was speechless.

That evening I began to map out a program of expanding activities, finding things to do that would perhaps allow Mike to discover some of the childhood experiences that had so totally eluded him. A few days later, I pointed to the pair of gigantic water tanks perched high on a bluff overlooking the main hospital.

"Would you like to hike up to those water tanks today, Mike?"

His gaze followed my arm, but his face remained blank.

"Water tanks, Mike. See those big green things up on that hill? That's where all the hospital water comes from. It's stored in those tanks until you turn on a faucet to get a drink, or when you see the sprinklers going, that's where the water comes from. You know about water faucets," I said and winked at him.

Mike's head bobbed. "Waduh, waduh, have hahn-doe?"

"No handles, Mike, you know better."

He nodded; he did indeed know better. Handles were a no-no for our kids. Normal youngsters will watch with intense concentration as pieces of wood or plastic boats float in a bathtub or down a gutter, but the child with schizophrenia will turn on a water tap full-blast and sit for hours mesmerized by it. So all the outdoor faucet handles at the hospital were kept locked when not in use. Mike had a well-earned reputation for spotting the spigot with an overlooked handle, then turning it on until someone discovered him. That's why he was wondering if those huge tanks had handles. He was anticipating releasing all that water.

"Do you want to hike up to the water tanks, Mike?"

An affirmative nod.

"Okay, ask me then. Hike up to the water tanks, Pat? Go ahead, say that."

"Hikup waduh tahnk . . . " a pause, ". . . Paht."

"Good! Very, very good, Mike!" I had been prepared to break the words up as I'd always done before, assuming that Mike wouldn't be able to put them together on his own. Now I realized that, even though his pronunciation was odd, the language was certainly there and available for development. It was a distinctly pleasant surprise, and all the more so because this was also the first time Mike had called me by name. I gave his scarecrow hair a rub. "And that was especially good because you said my name. What's my name, Mike?"

"Paht."

"Pat, Mike, say 'Pat,' not 'Pot.'"

"Paht."

"Pat. Say 'at.' Paaaat."

"Paht."

"Well okay, Mike," I sighed. I guessed I could get used to being called "Pot," although it had a certain questionable connotation. "Close enough, and an extra scoop of chocolate ice cream for you today."

So that afternoon we climbed to the water tanks. They were enormous, and once we had ascertained that there were no handles, Mike set about exploring the network of interlocking pipes that ran just above ground level between the two tanks. The water mains were huge two-foot-wide pipes and I quickly climbed one and tightroped across it. Mike watched me, openmouthed. Interspersed among the several mains was a series of smaller pipes and when I began balancing on them, he could restrain himself no longer. In

moments he had scrambled up beside me and, when I hung
by my knees and swung, his reaction was instantaneous.

"Me, me do! Paht, ME!"

"All right, sit like this." I slid off and put my hands on
his legs to steady him. "It's okay now, I have you, just keep
your legs curled around the pipe. There you go."

And there was Mike, hanging upside down, gently
swinging. We spent the next hour clambering among the
pipes, which made a nifty jungle gym. When we returned to
the cottage and I asked Mike to draw a picture of the tanks,
he jotted one right off. After that, the tanks became a regular
destination—and the subject of many drawings.

Over the months, Mike's pictures had multiplied expo-
nentially, and Jody suggested that he display some of them
on the bulletin board near the nursing station. Soon it was
filled and someone else prevailed upon Mike to transfer his
efforts to his own room. That appealed to him, and he
began to tape favorites to the cement block walls above his
bed.

After a few trips to the water tanks, I decided to try to capitalize on Mike's affinity for water by describing the filtration plant, located on the other side of the hospital grounds. We were walking through the parking lot and, after arousing his curiosity, I concluded with, "Lots of splashing water!" and spread my arms like the big circling aluminum booms. I stopped by my car. "Would you like to go to the water plant, Mike?"

He agreeably fell in with the plan. "Go waduh . . . " was as far as he got.

"Come over here, Mike." I knelt down in front of him. "Try this. Watch my lips. Water—"

"Waduh."

"No, try once more. Wa-*ter*."

Mike's expression was earnest and he was really trying, but although we went over this several more times, the "ter" sound was just too difficult for him.

"Okay. Now plant."

"Pwahnt."

"Close, try it again. Plant."

"Pwahnt."

I gave up; this was beyond him, too. Most of Mike's vowels were distorted, particularly "a," which usually came out "ah." "Okay, now try it together. Water plant."

"Waduh pwahnt."

"Good, buddy, that's close enough. Now we have only one other problem."

Mike picked up on my tone immediately and glanced sharply at me.

"We have to take my car. It's too far away to hike. How do you feel about going for a car ride with me, Mike?"

It had probably been years since he had been in one and

I wasn't sure how he'd react to this. He looked apprehensive, so I walked over to the car and opened the door.

"C'mon, Mike. A ride will be fun for you. We can go lots of places in the car. Especially the water plant. To see all the splashing water."

I got in and slid across to the driver's seat and then beckoned to Mike. He approached tentatively so I started the engine. "Last one in's a monkey's uncle, Mike!" I said, patting the seat beside me.

"Munng-key uhnn-koe."

"Right, come on."

After a brief hesitation, Mike climbed in and sat back stiffly against the seat. His head came barely to the bottom of the window so I told him to sit forward where he could see better. By the time we reached the main hospital grounds, Mike was craning his neck.

When we got to the filtration plant, I opened the door and he bounced out, eyes going wide as he spotted the water gushing out of the booms and cascading over the rocks. We walked around the massive pools and then climbed the catwalk that led to the plant. Stopping in front of a large control panel, Mike stared at the gauges, handles, and different colored lights.

A plant maintenance worker came over and, noticing Mike's interest, asked if he wanted to learn how to regulate the flow of water. Mike had moved closer to me as the man approached, but after I encouraged him he cautiously gripped the large wheel and rotated it slowly. When he grasped the connection between what he was doing and the increased water flow, he became euphoric. Spinning the wheel enthusiastically to the maximum output, he soon had the water splashing out of the pool.

"Waduh, waduh!!" he squealed.

The maintenance man moved in to shut the flow a bit. But Mike had a death grip on the wheel—he was in control and reveling in it.

"Easy, Mike," I counseled. "You're getting a little carried away. Turn it back down now."

But Mike wasn't having any of that, so I finally stepped over and cut the torrent to an acceptable level. Mike was acting goofy. His eyes dancing, he jumped up and down while holding tightly onto the wheel. I let him enjoy the ecstasy for a few moments, then said, "Okay, let the engineer take over, Mike, it's his turn."

I waited anxiously to see if he could relinquish his new acquisition. It was a struggle for him, but he finally backed away.

More comfortable now, the man said, "I'm going to give you a job here, Mike. Have to get you a hardhat like this." He took off his yellow hat and put it on Mike's head. "You like that?"

Mike nodded. This was almost more excitement than he could take.

"We'd better be going, Mike," I said.

"Come back anytime, Mike," urged the man. "My name is Ned. You can come and turn the valves and help me whenever you like."

Mike leaped at this offer. "Okay, come bahk tumawah!" he said emphatically, jumping again and clenching his fists into tight balls.

"Uhhh, Mike, slow down. Not tomorrow—but we will come back sometime soon. Give Ned back his hat and let's go." Turning, I thanked Ned for his patience; he couldn't have known how much this had meant to Mike.

As we headed for the car, Mike looked reluctantly over his shoulder at the splashing, rotating booms. He talked of little else for the next few days and later that week we returned.

With experiences like these, Mike's innate appetite for discovery began to flourish. Once opened, the curiosity and wonderment so typical of normal children spilled out as forcefully as the flow of that favorite industrial water valve. For the next couple of months we explored the entire hospital complex, thoroughly investigating every nook and cranny, all the little-known buildings, trails, and roads. There was also the hospital farm, which provided all the milk and eggs along with part of the meat for the hospital population. Initially frightened of the animals, Mike gradually learned to pet the cows and feed the chickens from his hand, yipping boisterously as they pecked his fingers.

And I continued to blend in teaching with our jaunts. The narrow road that led to the farm was lined with green pepper trees and an occasional gray- and titian-colored eucalyptus. I commented on the contrast one day and Mike pulled up, his attention caught by the unusual names. Pointing to a tree, he asked:

"Wha' tha' twee name?"

"That one's a pepper tree, Mike."

"Wha' tha' one ovuh deh?"

"That's a eucalyptus."

"Ah whaaat?!"

"Sit down for a second, Mike," I said, motioning him toward the curb. "Now watch my lips and say it after me. You—"

"Youuu—"

"Ca—"

"Caaaah—"

"Lip—"

"Wippp—" Mike was still having trouble pronouncing the "l" sound. And he tended to drop the ends of words; I purposely exaggerated the sound so he wouldn't swallow the last syllable.

"Tus!"

"Tisss!"

"Okay, now try it with me. Eu-ca-lip-tus."

"Eu-cah—"

"That's right, Mike. Eu-ca-lip-tus."

"Eu-ca-wip-tiss."

"Fine, good. Let's hear you say it by yourself now."

"Eucawip-tissss!"

"Very good, but we'll have to work some more on 'l'—luh—won't we? You know, this is a good idea, Mike. We'll start working on pronouncing words, maybe even while we're climbing on Dogface. Watch my lips again, Mike. Dog—"

"Dug—"

"Dauuuuuuugh, Mike. Open your mouth more and at the end say, 'gah!' Try it."

"Doooooogah—"

"Close. Good, try it again. Open wider. Like this. Dauuuuuugah—"

"Dauuuuuuu-gah!"

"Fine! That's perfect! Now say, 'fayyysss'—whistle the 's' between your teeth. Fayyysss—"

"Faaahs—"

"Fay*eeees*—"

"Faaahs."

"Good. Pretty close. Now put them together. Dogface."

"Dog-fahs!"

"Excellent, Mike." Half right, anyway. "Very good—you're getting it! That deserves a double-dip chocolate ice cream cone!"

He was excited when we reached the canteen and bounced up and down in front of the ice cream freezer considering other flavors before settling on his favorite. The rest of the afternoon was punctuated with Mike's intermittent chanting of the new sounds. Learning new words and their pronunciations was a game he liked and shortly thereafter I began taking a magazine along on our hikes. Whenever it was time for a rest, we would sit together and leaf through the pages, identifying pictures and practicing diction. The words retained a bizarre quality because of Mike's peculiar intonations and manner of delivery, but gradually his speech was becoming easier to understand.

There was no doubt that the severity of Mike's illness had left its residual marks. But unlike mental retardation, where intellectual development is constitutionally limited—and thus arrested at some level—schizophrenia poses no such boundaries. The only question was, how well would the psychological wounds heal? That and only that would determine how much Mike could achieve. One point was in his favor, though: everything to date seemed to indicate that he was a pretty bright kid.

As the months went by Mike became increasingly aware of what the other children were doing, what they did when they went on home visits—indeed, what home visits were—and what kinds of things they brought back. Soon Mike was asking me to bring him some of those goodies:

a box of animal crackers, his own crayons, a baseball cap.

Slowly the pathological behaviors dropped out. It was apparent that Mike's acknowledgment that all the people were looking the other way had been a key turning point. With that behind him, he began to accept the fact that some of us cared about him.

Cecile enthusiastically reported that he was more alert and beginning to take an interest in some of the classroom doings. And this new receptiveness was also carrying over to the cottage. Mike was calling Chuck "Chahk," and relating to others on the staff as well, asking a question here and there, coming closer, and generally testing the risky waters of relationships.

His solitary dance—the repetitive steps and ritualized syncopation—occurred much less frequently, then virtually disappeared. And so, the bud began to open. Gradually the silent Little Shadow began to explore a whole new world—a world in which he had existed but had never understood.

CHAPTER TEN

MY PHONE WAS BUZZING. INSISTENTLY. THAT WAS UN-
usual because I was seeing a family in therapy and the
secretary generally didn't interrupt. But she did now.

"Chuck from Mike's cottage is on line two—needs to
talk to you. Says it's urgent . . . "

"Okay, thanks." I punched the button, a queasy feeling
in the pit of my stomach. Had something happened to
Mike? Was he hurt? "Yes, Chuck. McGarry here."

"Doc, we got problems. Mike's dad showed up a little
while ago. He's acting pretty strange, says Mike's a lot better
so he wants to take him to church. Like right now. The minister wants to see Mike and pray over him. To get the
demons out or something like that. Mr. Harris won't take
no for an answer. Insists we sign Mike out to him right now.
I told him we got to talk with you first."

"Okay, I'll be over as soon as I finish up here."

"Uh, Doc . . . " Chuck's voice sounded huskier.

"Yeh?"

"Better get here as soon as you can. And brace yourself.

The old man's really been pressuring Mike and the little guy don't look so good. He's getting that spacy look again . . . "

"Okay, Chuck. Be right there. Thanks for warning me." As I hung up the phone I thought, Oh God, Mike, you sure didn't need this! Turning to the family, I explained that an emergency had arisen and that we would have to cut our session short. They were still nodding somberly as I raced from my office.

I had my key ready forty feet from the cottage, but Chuck was waiting, swinging the door open as I came up the walk.

"They're down in the dayroom." He closed the door and caught up with me. "It's gotten worse since I called."

I glanced at him questioningly.

"He's a different kinda guy."

"That's an understatement. What's he up to?"

"Seems to have a bug to take up where he left off four years ago. I don't know what in hell is going on with him. He just showed up, leaned on the buzzer 'til I let him in, and then when he saw Mike and how much better he seemed to be, he started telling him about all the things they were going to be doing together from now on. And first off is a visit to the minister, so he can pray for him! Now he's trying to get him to . . . well, you'll see for yourself. You won't believe it . . ."

By this time we were at the dayroom and I eased quietly through the door. Mike was crouched in the far corner, his eyes vacant. There was no recognition at all when I came in. He was scrunched down as if attempting to make the smallest possible target. His entire body was tensed for escape. What the hell *was* going on?

My eyes slowly left Mike and came to rest on Mr. Harris. He was down on both knees halfway across the room, his arms raised beseechingly toward Mike. He was so caught up in the fervor of his pleas that he didn't even see us come in.

"Tell Daddy you love him. Tell Daddy you love him, Michael; come here now, give me a big kiss and tell Daddy you love him. Please, Michael, tell Daddy . . . "

Chuck's whisper came over my shoulder. "That's what he's been doing for the last few minutes; nothing more about church. I think the guy's nuts."

Mike was staring vaguely in my direction and I tried to tell him with my eyes to hang on, I'd get him out of this fix. I was afraid of what was going on inside his mind. There was an unmistakably psychotic flavor to his expression; I hoped he wasn't retreating all the way back again. I approached his father and put my hand on his shoulder.

"Hello, Mr. Harris. Do you remember me? Patrick McGarry. Could we go to my office and talk, please?"

Silenced momentarily, he glanced back at my hand and then up at my face. There were tears trailing down both pasty white cheeks and his dazed eyes took a minute to focus on me. "He's my son," he said pleadingly.

"Yes, I know, Mr. Harris, but Mike isn't ready for this. It's too much, too fast. Now please, come with me."

He shook his head, turned away, and began to crawl toward Mike, resuming his appeal.

"Michael, tell Daddy you love him; please Michael, tell Daddy you love him—"

"Mr. Harris, stop it *right now!* This is very upsetting for Mike—he's not really able to tell you he loves you.

Now I want you to get hold of yourself and come with me. *Immediately."* My best authoritative tone was invoked. And ignored.

"Michael, come to Daddy, tell me you love me. Tell Daddy you care, you forgive him. Please Mikey, *tell me you love me!"* Mr. Harris's voice had become shrill, almost crackling with intensity.

There was something very wrong with him today; he was completely different from the man I had met several months earlier. That day he had at least been fairly rational, if hostile. A sudden thought froze me: maybe he's had a psychotic break, too. That'd make it three for three. I turned to Jody, who had just come into the room.

"See if you can reach Scott, or Conable. Quickly."

"Right." Jody took one look, nodded, and disappeared.

Mike remained crouched in the corner, but now he began to rock back and forth, his eyes closed, a staccato chatter emanating from deep in his throat. I didn't like the sound of that at all.

Hastily I stepped around Mr. Harris and bent over Mike. "Mike? It's Pat. I'm here now, it's okay."

No response.

I edged a bit closer. "Mike, it's okay now, there's nothing to be afraid of. Can you hear me, Mike?"

The rocking gait changed slightly, but that was all.

Suddenly Mr. Harris began to shout, "MICHAEL . . . TELL DADDY YOU LOVE HIM . . . TELL DADDY—"

Abruptly the chattering stopped. Mike's eyes opened wide in terror, his mouth making grotesque soundless movements and then, from his very depths, came a reverberating, chilling shriek. Mike screamed and screamed and when I moved to go near him he jumped away, hitting his head on a window handle. Blood began streaming down his face, into his eyes and around his mouth, but Mike was unaware of it. He just continued shrieking, clawing at himself, and leaving great welts on his cheeks.

Jody was back at my side again.

"I called Dr. Conable, he'll be up in a minute. We'll have to sedate Mike. That gash looks like it'll need stitches."

I nodded numbly, glancing at Mr. Harris. I couldn't believe everything had been dismantled so quickly by this screwball. The dumb son of a bitch! What in hell was he thinking? Appearing out of the blue and pulling all this stuff on his son—after he'd abandoned him for four years!

Jody must have been reading my mind. "Be cool," she said softly.

"Yeh, sure," but my voice was tight. It was a fight for control.

Moments later, Conable and an entourage of aides joined us. As the aides moved in to assist, he was on their heels, pointing a mean-looking syringe in the air.

"Hold him still," he said and the aides closed in, but they weren't really needed. Jody had edged in ahead of them, speaking soothingly as she reached out and took Mike's arm. His eyes were tightly closed, as if he were expecting to be struck. He flinched when she touched him, but astonishingly made no attempt to get away. Still talking reassuringly, Jody unbuckled Mike's pants and bared a buttock. He scarcely moved as the needle penetrated and in less than a minute he slumped into her waiting arms. Almost immediately she was applying pressure to his head, blotting the blood with a piece of gauze, consoling Mike even after he was knocked out by the powerful sedative.

I was standing by, a bit in shock, and feeling totally helpless.

Conable looked over at me. "Why don't you see what you can do for him." He nodded toward Mike's father, and I could tell by his tone that he wasn't too pleased about all this, either.

Mr. Harris was still on his knees, leaning on a nearby stool, his head and shoulders sagging.

"Come with me please, Mr. Harris." This time I wasn't about to be ignored, but he offered no resistance. I lifted him to his feet and steered him down the hall and into the small anteroom behind the nursing station. Dazed and remote himself, he sat silently, tears streaming down his cheeks.

Then he began praying, softly at first. "Dear God, I just don't understand any of this. Whatever went wrong with my son is absolutely beyond me. I'll never understand why you did this to us—we never hurt nobody, we've led good Christian lives. What did we ever do to be punished like this? My only son . . . only *child* . . . and I don't even know him." He shook his head. "I've *never* known him. Oh God, why have you forsaken us like this? Why, why?"

Abruptly he began to sob, and all I could do was sit and listen to his grief spill out. In a sense he was right; it was almost as if the family *had* been cursed. Sorrow, sickness, and pain had certainly riddled their lives. My anger at what he had done began to abate. He was a person in deep trouble himself, another of life's walking wounded. Finally, the sobbing subsided and, his eyes avoiding mine, his voice hesitant, he began again.

"Mikey seemed so much better to me today. But I'll bet you're going to say I've ruined everything now . . . "

"Well, we'll just have to wait and see, Mr. Harris. But in any event, you should have checked with us before coming up here so that we could have prepared Mike for your visit. It's been a few years, after all."

Mike's father recoiled, perhaps realizing for the first time how long it had been. He seemed compelled to justify his absence.

"Well, since your visit a while back, Mike has been very much in our thoughts—and in our prayers. But like I told you, when we brought him here he wouldn't even come near us, talk to us. It just hurt so bad, having a child who was a stranger to us. It was more than either my wife or I could handle. Especially my wife. It was all just too much for her." He ran a hand anxiously over his forehead and cleared his throat. "I took her to the mental health center like you suggested. She had the worst spell ever . . . came home and found her like in a trance or something . . . just staring at the TV—but it wasn't on. And she didn't even recognize me. That scared me plenty I can tell you. . . . She's better now since we've been going to the clinic twice a month. They put her on some sort of medicine."

"I'm glad to hear that, Mr. Harris."

"We've talked to them about Mike, too. It hasn't been easy. Have you any idea how you feel about yourself when your own son has to be shut up in a mental hospital?"

I shook my head. After a moment, I asked, "What made you decide to come out today?"

"Well, like I say, we've been praying for Mike every day now. Ever since you dropped by. Praying that he'll recover and be released. And we talk regularly with our minister and the social worker. But we have a new minister now, and he suggested that maybe we should bring Mike to church so that the devils that are inside him could be cast out. They're the ones—Satan, that is—who've done this to him. He's demon-possessed, you know!" Suddenly Mr. Harris's expression began to harden again, his voice becoming more charged, his eyes burning. It was the fanatical Mr. Harris threatening to emerge. But then he caught himself and looked sharply at me.

"I know you prob'ly don't believe in demon possession. You think I'm a crackpot, but that's what's happened to our little Mikey, and nobody is going to tell me *any different!*" His fist hit with a *whap* against his open palm to emphasize the point. Mr. Harris was cranking up again.

I raised my hand. "You're certainly entitled to your beliefs—"

"It doesn't matter," he interrupted, cutting me off. "Anyway, I came up to see Mike by myself, to see if I could take him to church. I thought it'd be too hard on Mother, she'd get too upset, so I came alone. And then when I saw how much better Mikey was when I got here, that he didn't run away like he used to, that he even talked to me—I thought he was cured, the demons had finally been driven out after all these years. It seemed like a miracle, a sign. I thought Satan had finally been beaten. And I rejoiced and thanked God . . .

"But then when I wanted to pray with Mike, to embrace him, he ran into the corner and no matter how hard I tried to tell him I love him, he wouldn't speak to me again or let me near him. Just like before. When he began screaming and hitting himself again—" Mr. Harris's voice caught, choked, and he sighed, "I guess I was wrong, it was too much to expect. I just don't get it, how he can change so quickly. One second he's fine and the next . . . "

"Would you like to begin trying to understand, Mr. Harris? And help Mike, too?"

He looked up sharply. "What do you mean?"

"I simply mean that Mike is," I paused, correcting myself, "*was* making real progress, and I hope he will again. But what would help immeasurably would be if he had a mother and father who would love him, show him that love, and at the same time gain some understanding of the serious emotional problems he has."

"Well of course we love him," Mr. Harris broke in. "We care about him very much, he knows that! We've told him enough."

"But because of his illness," I suggested carefully, "he just hasn't been in a position to accept or return that love. And still isn't, although he was getting better. But it'll take time before he'll be able to do that. I would suggest, though, that you and your wife continue in counseling and come up here occasionally, meet with me, visit with Mike, and perhaps in time Mike may once again be the child you love and have prayed for."

Mr. Harris stared at his hands and said nothing. So I went on:

"I guess we all want the same thing—to see Mike get better and be able to leave the hospital. Maybe we can combine our forces toward that end?"

I thought I detected a trace of interest. I was throwing Mr. Harris a rope and he couldn't decide whether to grab it or not.

"I'll consider your suggestion, but let me ask you a couple of questions."

I nodded. "Shoot."

"Are you a Christian? Do you read the Bible every day? Or are you one of those educated liberals who've destroyed the faith in what used to be a God-fearing country?"

"Well, Mr. Harris, I don't want to seem evasive, but my

religious beliefs really have nothing to do with my work. All I'm concerned about is seeing that Mike and kids like him get the kind of treatment they need so they can leave here and get along on the outside and, with a little luck, lead fairly happy and healthy lives. That's the main thing. Isn't that what all of us are interested in?"

"Yeh, I suppose it is. But your religious background is mighty important. Don't ever underestimate how it influences your entire life, and the lives of everybody you come in contact with. The Lord is all-powerful, merciful to His flock, but you must repent your sins and accept Him as your Savior." His voice had taken on the cadence of a television evangelist.

"That may be true for you," I conceded. "I think I'm a deeply religious person, although I don't identify with any particular belief or church—Christianity, Judaism, or even Buddhism, for that matter. I guess I believe in parts of all of them."

Mr. Harris's eyebrows shot up. "Even Buddhism?" He pronounced it "Budism."

"Yes, especially Buddhism," I went on, undaunted. "And I couldn't tell you the last time I read the Bible because I honestly don't remember, but I *can* tell you that I don't think it's as important that a person read the Bible every day as it is that he abides by its principles." I met his scorching eyes straight on. "If you insist on categorizing me, I guess I'd be considered a humanist. My concern is for people, their welfare, their well-being. Especially those with psychological disorders. If you equate being liberal with making people's lives better, I'm all for it—but I certainly don't consider humanism, or liberalism for that matter, responsible for the problems our country is having—"

"So, you're not a God-fearing man?" Mr. Harris seemed to be pressing for some kind of surrender.

"No, I'm not, Mr. Harris. I can't relate to a God who would put demons in people—especially little boys—or punish them and inflict them with pain and suffering. People do that to people, nature makes mistakes, bad karma intervenes—there are all kinds of ways of explaining the illnesses, the suffering in this world. But I don't hold God responsible. So for what it's worth, I am a believer in God. I just don't fear Him. I fear destructive human qualities far more—greed, hatred, prejudice, cruelty . . . "

Mr. Harris's expression did not soften.

"Well, do I pass the test, Mr. Harris?"

"I'll think it over, what you suggested. We'll see, but I'm not promising anything."

"Fine. As long as you're willing to consider becoming more involved with Mike, that's all he, or I, could ask. Maybe we can combine the best of both our beliefs."

For that rejoinder I got a sharp, frank look.

"Well," Mr. Harris finally relented a bit, "I don't have much of an education, but I know you're trying to help Mike. Could you let me and the Mrs. know how he is from time to time?"

"Sure, Mr. Harris, I'll be glad to."

Later on that afternoon, I walked back over to Mike's cottage. A couple of nurses were conversing in the nursing station and both turned as I approached. I didn't even have to ask.

"Dr. Conable was up a little while ago and ordered another shot for Mike. Wants him knocked out for a while, hoping it'll minimize the aftereffects."

"Probably a good idea. I guess I'll just go down and see him for a few minutes."

"If there's anything we can do—"

"No, thanks anyway. Nothing anyone can do until we see how Mike comes out of this."

When I reached his room Mike was lying on his back, the deep regular breathing of sedation broken by an occasional tiny snore that made me smile. His cut had been bandaged, the white gauze encircling his head, his lopped-off blond hair protruding here and there in clumps. I tried to read from his expression what might happen, but without seeing his eyes, knowing whether they would be averted or not, it was impossible to tell anything. So I just sat on the edge of the bed and, in the half-light, tried to come to terms with the events of the day, and why such things had to happen to those least able to defend themselves. It all seemed terribly unfair.

Mike's leg began to twitch under the blanket, as if he were trying to run, and I rested my hand on it, giving it a few pats. Involuntarily, I spoke what I was thinking:

"You're going to be okay, little buddy. We've come too far together to let anything separate us now. I promise you, Mike, we'll work this out, too. You can count on it." Mike stirred, and the twitching stopped. Then the deep measured breathing resumed. Tucking the blanket up around his neck, I murmured, "See you tomorrow, Monkey's Uncle."

In the parking lot I ran into Scott. He had been conducting a workshop down on the main grounds all day, so I hadn't seen him since early morning. But I could sense his concern as he came up to me.

"Heard about what happened. Pretty grim, huh?"

"Yeh. Very." I didn't feel very much like talking about it just yet.

"How did Harris know where Mike was?"

"One of the kids told him, so he just bypassed us."

"Ahhh, yes. That figures. Did you have a chance to talk with him?"

"Sort of. He's really an unstable guy. Anything bad that can't be explained is the work of the devil. But at least they've been getting some counseling since I saw him last. And he says Mrs. Harris is on medication now."

"Hmmm. How's Mike?"

"Not good, Scott, not good at all."

Aware of my reluctance to go into it, Scott said, "Well, we'll talk about it tomorrow. Anything I can do now?" he offered.

"Not really. Thanks anyway. I guess this sort of thing just comes with the territory. Under the circumstances, all you can do is keep your fingers crossed and hope for the best. Right?"

Scott nodded. "I'm afraid so. There's always going to be that element of uncertainty. You've done what you can and now you have to wait and see what develops. You have to learn to deal with situations like this."

"Yeh . . ."

"Take it easy now, Pat. Go on home and relax. We'll talk about it tomorrow."

CHAPTER ELEVEN

THAT NIGHT I GAVE SOME HARD THOUGHT TO MY CHOSEN profession. It was amazing how tangled up you could get with a kid. It was almost as if Mike had become my own child, but I hadn't realized until now just how much of an emotional investment I had in him. Now I was suddenly, acutely, aware of it.

I wondered if my attachment were impairing—would impair—the effectiveness of my work. A therapist inevitably has an emotional stake in his patients, particularly those he works with for any length of time. But he also has to remain objective and relatively detached. And yet with kids it just seemed so much more difficult not to become overinvolved. Where did you draw the line? It was something I needed to discuss with Scott.

I lay in bed, the events of the day on replay in my mind. I kept wondering if there were anything I could have, should have, done differently. And wondering, too, what the outcome would be.

It wasn't until after midnight that I finally fell asleep,

and even then, as tired as I was, I slept badly. Finally, at half-past five, I gave it up. I needed to get out to the hospital and see what was going on.

By the time I arrived at the cottage, the ward personnel were waking the children and herding them down the corridor to the bathroom. It was by far the earliest I'd ever been there. This was a part of hospital routine I'd missed. I paused outside Mike's room and listened for any sounds from within, but I could hear nothing. Then, pushing the door slightly, I stepped inside. Mike was lying on his side, staring at the wall.

"Mike? Hi, how're you doing?"

There was no response from him, not even a slight movement. The vacant eyes were fastened to the cement block wall. I started to move toward the bed, but then stopped when Mike began curling up into a little ball, drawing the blanket over his head.

"Mike? It's Pat—your buddy."

A small hand clenched the blanket even more tightly. It was all I could see; the rest of him was a motionless lump.

"Mike, are you okay? Can we talk about it, buddy? I won't come near if you don't want me to, but try and talk with me, okay?"

There was no reaction.

I pulled up the only chair and sat quietly for a while, thinking it would be better if I didn't push him right now. He'd been pushed enough yesterday. But after ten minutes of silence, I decided to try for some response, even just a tiny one. So that I'd know everything we'd worked so hard for wasn't irretrievably lost.

"Mike, I'm going to leave now. But do me one favor? Just stick out your finger and wiggle it a little. I need to know

that my buddy's okay. Would you do that for me? Just
wiggle a finger, Mike . . . "

Nothing. No movement at all. I waited several more
minutes, but he remained rigidly still.

I sighed. "I'll be back in a while, Mike. You rest up
some more and take it easy. See you later."

I walked back to the nursing station and wrote a brief
note, detailing Mike's behavior. I asked the duty nurse to
let him stay in bed for the time being, but if he did get up,
or say anything, to track me down right away. Then I slowly
wended my way to my office. Scott's secretary was just getting in and I asked her when he would have some time.

"Not till 11:30 at the earliest, I'm afraid."

"Okay, put me down."

I was busy myself all morning, but toward eleven the
phone buzzed.

"McGarry."

"Jody here. I've got some good news . . . and some bad
news . . . "

"Give me the good first."

"Mike's up, and he had something to eat. *But,* he won't
get dressed, won't let anyone near him, won't speak to anyone, and—" Jody paused and sighed, "he's back to the stork
steps, all the magical rituals and stuff again."

"Damn." My worst fears were confirmed. "Okay,
thanks, Jody. Keep me posted, will you please?"

"Sure. Sorry, Pat, I guess we start over now."

After I hung up, I did some of my own staring out the
window, trying to bring some understanding to it all. The
gains Mike had made had been extraordinary, but there
really hadn't been the opportunity to integrate them before
the old man showed up. What timing!

Scott interrupted my reverie as he paused outside my

door. "Bring your cup and come next door for a bit, huh?" he suggested. "You look like a man who could use some therapy . . . "

"I heard how Mike is—now tell me how you are."

"Not bad, I guess, all things considered. Spent a lot of time last night, though, wondering if there were anything I could have done differently—wishing that I had just picked Harris up and booted him out the door . . . "

"But he *is* Mike's father—"

"Yeh, I know . . . some father. Mike was doing fine without him."

"I gather you were pretty angry with him?"

"Understatement of the year, but a good counseling reflection anyway!" I laughed. Scott looked a bit sheepish at being called on one of his therapeutic gambits. "Yeh, I was mad as hell at him. Still am. I lay awake most of last night thinking about it. Does this kind of thing happen very often, Scott?"

"Setbacks? Monkey wrenches in the works? Unfortunately, yes. It's one of the more common problems, especially when you work with children. You have to be very careful—particularly with the parents. Sometimes the whole family is locked into a scapegoating action; they've targeted one person—perhaps the most independent child—and everybody unloads on the kid. It's the therapist's job to help the family see that, and it's easy to get caught in the middle. Then, of course, the family dumps on you. Or worse yet, as the kid gets better, the parents, or the family, undercut you."

"Do you think that's what's happening with Mike's father? Is he going to try and sandbag us as Mike gets better?"

"It's hard to say. I don't think so; people don't consciously plan such sabotage. But he's been out of the picture so long it may be difficult for him to cope with Mike's improvement. Things like that do happen."

I was making little church steeples with my fingers, probably in deference to Mr. Harris. I couldn't quite voice what I was thinking and we sat in silence for a few moments. It was a hard thing for me to talk about, to put into words. Finally I began,

"You know, last night I really had trouble with this. To paraphrase one of our famous predecessors, I know I was never promised a rose garden, but I really feel terrible about Mike. I've been brooding over everything from his tenuous hold on reality to my equally tenuous hold on being a competent psychotherapist. And now, after yesterday, the futility of it all. I don't know, it's a hell of a time to find this out, but I think I get too caught up—overinvolved—and then, when the disappointment hits, the bottom drops out. Do you know what I mean?"

All I could read in Scott's expression was support; he didn't seem appalled by what I felt was a crushing admission. He nodded and then reached for his favorite briar. It took him a few seconds to get it stoked, and then he said, "Well, Pat . . . I can't give you the answer to that. No one can. My experience has been that each therapist has to work this out—for himself, or herself. It's part of the price we pay for being in the trenches. And you can imagine what happens when you're following two dozen or more patients in therapy. The responsibilities are very demanding, and put fantastic pressure on you. You're involved, concerned, taking risks with depressed and suicidal patients, violence-prone ones, you name it. Last week when I let Amy go on a home visit, I worried all weekend, jumped every time the phone rang . . . "

Amy was a twelve-year-old who had seriously tried to kill herself a half-dozen times, the last one with rat poison. It had burned away much of her stomach, leaving what remained ulcerated and constantly painful. It was a miracle she'd survived.

"But we can't just lock her up in Merrick for the rest of her life," Scott went on. "I had to take a chance sometime, hope that I understood her and the family well enough to know that she had improved to the point that I could risk it. But," he sighed, "that didn't make it any easier."

"So you never really do learn to live with the pressure?"

"Oh, I think you come to terms with it. But being a psychotherapist *is* a high-risk job, and some times are worse than others. As we've talked about, people are not exactly predictable. They'll make demands, sometimes excessive ones, and you have to deal with it. Other times, a person seems to be doing exceptionally well and then all of a sudden everything falls apart. An unexpected psychotic break, a suicide attempt, maybe even successful, and everything crashes around you. That's why you have to learn to be tough-minded—and yet retain your sensitivity. Otherwise," Scott paused and drew hard on his pipe, "otherwise, you don't last. You burn out. Become indifferent to the plight of your patients or perhaps shield yourself with a harsh, nononsense style of therapy. Or—as some psychiatrists have been known to do—you become a pill-pusher, keeping the patient in a chemical straitjacket, so you never have to get around to doing deep, intensive psychotherapy. There are all kinds of escapes. Some people just opt out, become administrators or program directors, which cuts down their exposure to patients. The trend now is to try and spread yourself out a bit, maybe do some teaching, a little consulting, along with a therapy practice. The trick is to find a balance that suits you."

He leaned forward, tapping his pipe against the side of an ashtray. "But you see, Pat, situations like what occurred yesterday, and worse, are bound to happen, perhaps make you question the steps you took or whether there wasn't something else you could have done. We come back to the experience variable: knowing as much as you can about how human beings behave in certain situations, making the best professional judgment you can at the time, evaluating it afterward, and filing it away for future reference."

We sat in silence for a while. One other disturbing thought kept recurring, but I couldn't bring myself to say it aloud. Scott was watching me, an almost mellow softness to his expression; the concern for his star pupil was genuine and I knew it.

"Say it," he urged gently.

"Say what?"

"What you're thinking."

"Oh, Jesus, Scott. You damn psychologists, always reading people's minds."

Scott waited patiently.

"I don't know if I can express it or not. It's very difficult for me to admit."

"Try."

"Well, . . . you know what's going through my mind with all this. I mean, . . . maybe I'm just not cut out to be a psychotherapist. Maybe I'm not strong enough to ride the cutting edge, shoulder all the responsibilities, the disappointments, the upsets, the setups, the setbacks, you name it. God, I don't know what in hell I'd do if a patient ever suicided on me. Here I am coming unglued over Mike, but what would happen if someone in my care *killed* himself? If I were seeing a kid like Amy and she did herself in and it was my responsibility . . . God, that'd be hard to live with. . . . "

"All we can do is try, Pat. But you know, we don't have control over people's lives. Responsibility, yes—to a point. We do what we can to help others, but we can go just so far. The choice for what they do is theirs. Even suicide. If someone is determined to kill himself, there may be nothing we or anyone else can do to prevent it. But although we may feel a sense of responsibility when that happens—and agonize over whether we might have been able to turn things around if we'd just been more alert, more sensitive . . . in the end what it comes down to is that each person bears the ultimate responsibility for his own actions."

"I can accept that rationally, Scott. But how to deal with the *feelings* inside is the problem. . . . I just don't know. . . . "

Scott leaned back in his chair. "I guess the key is time. And with time comes experience. That will bring a certain measure of objectivity that allows you to monitor your feelings, your empathy. So that you'll know when to detach yourself, and pull back."

"Well, to be honest with you, I'm seriously questioning whether I'll ever be able to do that."

"There's only one way to find out, though, and you're doing it. You'll have doubts—the most natural thing in the world. There'd be something wrong with you if you didn't. But don't hold yourself accountable for too much. Just give yourself time, step back, keep your perspective, and use me. That's what I'm here for."

"Thanks, Scott." The weight of self-doubt had begun

to lift and I felt almost cheerful. I couldn't believe it. "You know, you're a hell of a therapist!"

Scott shrugged, still serious. "Promise me one thing, though?"

"Sure."

"When you get into tough situations—and I can guarantee you that you will—use your colleagues. They're your friends. They'll understand the turmoil, the confusion, because they've experienced it, too. And you may have to help a few of them at times; it's reciprocal. As I said before, this is a high-risk business. There's a lot of stress—that's why we play up the team treatment concept. It's mutually supportive—we lean on each other. It diffuses things a bit when we know we can reach out to someone else if we have to, that there's no need for us to bear the whole weight ourselves. No one really can, you know."

"Yeh. This is quite a profession we're in."

"Nothing like it. It's not for everyone. But someone has to take care of the Amys, the Mikes, the Dannys of the world. As rough as it is sometimes, *someone* has to do it. . . . "

Later, sitting in my cubbyhole office, I was staring out the window, my mind idling in neutral, when I noticed Mike's folder at the top of the stack. The secretary must have left it there. A progress note was due. Good timing; I'd have a mouthful for this dictation.

Picking up the file, I leafed through the pages, smiling ironically as I read the frustration that flowed from between the lines of my earlier notes. The Good Old Days. Or were they so good? Actually, they had been pretty grim. Back then I hadn't seen a sign of anything encouraging. I was surprised all over again by how much progress Mike had made and how much there now was to build on. What the hell was I getting so discouraged for? Impulsively, I picked up the phone and dialed.

"Cottage 4, Fletcher."

"Jody, Pat here. When you have a chance, would you tell Mike I'll be up in a little while for our hike on Dogface. Even if he doesn't seem to hear you, say it to him a number of times."

"Okay, I'll tell him. But he's still out of it. No change."

"Yeh, I know, but I've got to try something."

"Okay."

Shortly after two o'clock that afternoon, I took a seat on a low table in the dayroom across from the hunched form near the window. Mike had his back to me. He still had his pajamas on.

"Mike, this is a special occasion. It's a beautiful day, and I'm ready for a hike up Dogface. How about you? You don't have to draw any pictures or even ask for the hike. This is your day. Whatever you want to do, buddy, we'll do . . ."

There was no movement, just the rhythmic breathing reflected through the back of his thin pajama top.

"C'mon, Mike, get dressed, put on your hiking boots, and let's get out of this old cottage for a while. It's a nice day and I'll bet the views are great at the top of Dogface. Maybe we could stop for some pop or a chocolate ice cream cone on the way back if you want. It's your day!"

I tried a few more times to engage him, but there was no response at all and gradually my hopes for a speedy remission dwindled. It was going to be a long way home.

I pulled up a chair across the room, where I thought Mike's peripheral vision would include me. Then we sat quietly, listening to the rhythm of the cottage: periodic loudspeaker pagings, the occasional peal of a child's laughter, screams, or shouts that drifted into the room. There were some things that I thought needed saying; I'd just gamble that he would be tuned in enough to hear some of them.

"Mike, let me try and explain a little bit about what happened yesterday. First of all, I think your father felt very bad about how hard he pushed you and about what he caused. He just didn't understand what you've been through, how difficult it's been for you. And I guess when he first saw you, he wanted to believe that everything was all right, that somehow or other all the problems of the past had just gone away. He didn't realize how you've been struggling with things, trying to understand yourself and other people. Or how sometimes things hurt inside. Yesterday, you saw your father confused by it all. Like you have been at times. You've been trying to understand new words, new things, and it's been confusing for you, and very scary. Right?"

Mike continued to gaze blankly out the window. I had no idea whether he heard what I was saying. But I pressed on.

"I don't know what you're feeling inside right now, Mike, but let me guess. Yesterday, when your father asked you to do things you just couldn't do, you must have been really frightened. And then when you saw him getting so upset, it was even more scary for you. So now you're afraid of all of us again, afraid that we'll be expecting you to say or do things that you're not ready for yet. And the only way you have of protecting yourself is to close us out again. But everyone—especially your father—is truly sorry for what happened. We all feel very bad about it, especially because you've been trying so hard lately to understand yourself and

all those scary feelings inside. We can't change what happened, but I want you to know that we won't ask you to do
anything until you feel ready for it. So the next step is up to
you. But we're hoping you'll give us another chance, Mike.
Okay?"

I stayed with him for over an hour, but I might as well
have been by myself. He had pulled way back again. The
wall, which had so spectacularly toppled during the last few
months, had been as spectacularly rebuilt overnight.

The next day, and the day after that, I went up to the
cottage to sit with Mike, occasionally saying something to
him, but generally just sharing the minutes of heavy, porten-
tous silence. Usually he was in the dayroom rocking or
moving to the synchronized beat of his solitary dance, his
eyes empty, unseeing. When meals were called, the beat
would stop and Mike marched mechanically out of the cottage and down the path, staying as far away from the other
kids as possible, scrupulously inspecting each step to the
dining hall. Apart from this, he showed absolutely no
interest in leaving the cottage, much less hiking on Dogface
or going to the canteen. He had become a thoroughly
remote figure once again—even more so than before—and
the staff, respecting his plight, made allowances.

I went up to see him every day that week. Friday was a
particularly beautiful day, and I tried to tempt him with a
hike, or a trip to the water plant, even a short walk. But it
was all for naught. His mind was turned away and whatever
recesses he had taken refuge in were not open to my pleas.
He was on a totally different wavelength.

Nothing changed the following week. Each afternoon I
prepped myself for another inspirational message to Mike,

trod the path to the cottage, delivered my speech, sat in prolonged silence, and finally departed. I could sense the frustration creeping in, the edginess returning, the doubts resurfacing. I kept telling myself, I got through before, I can do it again. There's got to be an answer, there's got to be a way to reach him. But what is it? Where is it?

A few weeks later, I had a flareup with Dr. Conable. He had been switching and adjusting Mike's medications in an attempt to stabilize him but it hadn't made any difference and the staff had reluctantly agreed that Mike had regressed back to his former state. I hadn't contributed much during the review meeting, but just as I was about to urge that the staff should be patient and not assume the worst, to give Mike a bit more time, Conable closed Mike's metal chart with a snap.

"I'm afraid Mike Harris is beyond reach. There's nothing else I can think of in the way of chemotherapy. Maybe a shock treatment or two would do something. It might be worth a try. After all, he's practically catatonic."

An uneasy silence settled over the room. Conable glanced up from the next chart he had opened, sensing that something was wrong. His eyes fell warily on me.

"That's bullshit!" I exploded. "That would drive Mike so far back in he'd *never* come out!" I could sense that my face had flushed.

No one spoke and an uncomfortable silence stretched out. It was Debbie Shaw who came to the rescue. "I think Pat is right. Shock treatments are pretty extreme. We have other options before we consider anything like that."

Several others quickly voiced their agreement.

"Well, we can wait," Conable said in a more conciliatory tone. He obviously had not expected such a strong reaction from me or so much resistance from the staff. "That's the absolute last resort, of course, and not something we'd ordinarily do with a child. But it may eventually come to that. . . . "

Someone hastily brought up another youngster who had been causing problems lately and the discussion moved on. From across the room, I shot a look of gratitude at Debbie and she smiled back. I owed her one.

After the meeting Conable and I apologized to each other. He admitted that his judgment was premature and, in any event, bad form when someone else's patient was involved. I grudgingly acknowledged that there might be some validity to his remark that Mike was beyond reach. At this point, I wasn't being terribly objective.

When I got back to my apartment late that afternoon, I made a nice, very-limey gimlet and, adding the makings for another to the frosty shaker, headed for the deck. Savoring that tangy first sip, rolling it around while my mouth puckered, I nestled into the chaise and considered the upcoming weekend. Tomorrow I'd go down to the beach and do a little surfing. That always cleared my head. Maybe catch a movie in the evening; some diversion might help. I watched the sun sink slowly into the ocean, waiting for the merciful withdrawal of the tension sword that had been embedded between my shoulder blades all week.

CHAPTER TWELVE

ANOTHER WEEK PASSED, WHICH MADE FIVE SINCE MR. Harris's visit. I hadn't heard from him, but then I really didn't expect him to reappear; he'd probably fade away again. Often during this time my mind would replay the whole incident. Mike's face—his total reversion—would fill the screen, and the anger toward Mr. Harris for what he had done would burn a little deeper. Finally, late one morning I rolled the chair back from my desk and said aloud, "The hell with it. I've got to get out of this nuthouse for a while."

I changed into my Levi's and hiking boots, which I hadn't bothered to wear for the last few weeks, grabbed my lunch, and took to the hills. On my way, I decided to stop at the cottage and give Mike the chance to go with me. He was in the dayroom he preferred, doing his rocking routine, so engrossed that he didn't notice me. Nor did he slow when I spoke.

"I need a break and I'm going to hike up Dogface, Mike. You've been cooped up here for over a month now, and so have I. If you'd like to come along, you're welcome to. I'm leaving right now and since no one else is here, the door will be open for a few minutes if you decide you want to go with me."

Without waiting to see what, if anything, he'd do, I turned and walked down the corridor to the outside door and opened it. Fortunately, most of the kids were off having lunch and the ward was virtually deserted. I asked Chuck to watch for Mike and lock the door again if it didn't look as if he were going to leave. When I reached the hole, I peered out from behind the bushes. The door to Cottage 4 was shut again and there was no sign of Mike on the quad.

As I approached the foothills, my mood began to clear. Following a side trail, I decided to detour around by the old riverbed, laboring through the sand for a quarter of a mile before climbing up the clay walls to find a game path that led toward Dogface.

Periodically shifting my brown-bag lunch between my perspiring hands, I stopped every now and then to sniff the pungent aroma of the manzanita bushes that thrived in the rocky soil. The undergrowth dwindled as I gained elevation and came at last to the familiar trail, the one that led to the lemon orchard. Soon the fragrant trees came into sight and a short time later I reached the grove. Crossing through it, I paused on the far side and leaned against a boulder to catch my breath before beginning the ascent up Dogface.

I was mopping my brow when, beyond the orchard and down along the brush line, a movement caught my eye. Maybe it was a deer; Mike and I had glimpsed them on occasion and once we had even seen the swift flash of a red fox. I watched the spot intently, hoping to catch sight of the creature.

And then a flapping checkered shirt darted out from a

line of scrub. Moments later a slight figure entered the grove, head down, moving purposefully. He glanced briefly at a nearby lemon tree, but then came directly toward me.

It was Mike! Quickly I wheeled and began hiking swiftly up the trail, away from him. As I climbed, I marveled and exulted. He must have sneaked out of the cottage and hidden behind the building until I'd gone through the fence, because there wouldn't have been anywhere for him to hide once he cut across the quad. And he had caught up with me now because he'd taken our usual trail, the quickest way to the top. Maybe, just maybe, the lure of Dogface was going to start opening Mike up again. It was difficult to resist the urge to turn around to see how far back he was. But the voice of reason and caution rose inside me, counseling: Stay cool, don't get your hopes up! Push on ahead, let things develop as they will, let Mike call the shots.

I could feel the exhilaration when I reached the crest of Dogface and settled on the rock that had become my regular perch. One idea chased another through my mind as I rested there. Maybe Mike was back to his shadowing days, when he had followed people from a distance. But even that would be a vast improvement over his recent exile—the chance for another beginning. From the slope behind me came the sound of his boots scraping against the rocks and loose gravel. I tensed, but continued to gaze out over the valley while the anticipation roiled around inside me. And then Mike was striding past me not five feet away, his face set in firm resolution as I greeted him.

"Hey, Mike, you decided to come along after all."

He halted, head down, intent on arranging some pebbles with the toe of his boot. His stock monotone, with its equally familiar refrain, announced, "Hike up Dogfahs." Then Mike turned and marched over to his rock, seated himself and, taking a deep breath, assumed his all-encompassing ritual surveillance across the misty valleys toward the silvery ocean in the distance.

I said nothing more. The cool sea breezes were sweeping up the foothills today and farther north, along the coast, a fog bank seemed set on recapturing the shoreline. It was enough just to sit together for a while and let the beautiful vista do its own form of healing. That might be the kind of therapy Mike needed most now. I was determined to be patient, let him make the next move, and just be there if he needed me. Gradually, his expression softened and the harsh, guarded, crazy quality subsided.

Suddenly it occurred to me that I was hungry and I remembered my lunch. Mike certainly hadn't had time to eat, either. The bag rustled as I opened it and unwrapped a bologna sandwich. Tearing it in half, I looked up to see Mike staring at it.

"Would you like part of my sandwich, Mike? Hikers have to eat well. Here . . . " and I stretched the bigger half toward him, hoping the light breeze would give him a good whiff.

It did and Mike couldn't resist. He fairly leaped off the rock, grabbed the sandwich from my hand, and began wolfing it down.

"Hey, easy there, Mike. Nobody's going to take it away from you. Haven't they been feeding you?"

Mike continued to devour it noisily, his eyes following my movements as I poured some iced tea from the thermos into its cap.

"Want something to drink?"

He nodded eagerly, but never stopped chewing as he took the cup from my hand. Downing the tea in huge loud gulps, he thrust the cup back at me.

I laughed and shook my head. "More tea? It's good, huh?"

He nodded absently, intent on the sandwich again as I poured him a second cup of tea. When my half of the sandwich was almost gone, I said, "You want my last bite? It's a little present for being such a good friend and coming up here today."

Mike took the sandwich remnant and half of the orange I had peeled.

"Tastes good when we can sit on Dogface and have a picnic, doesn't it, Mike? We should do it again. Would you like that?"

An emphatic nod.

"Good, we'll do again real soon. And Mike . . . it's really great to have my hiking buddy with me again. I want you to know that. I missed you."

Mike glanced over at me and our eyes met. I saw the trust. We relaxed for a while then before it was time for me to get back. Eventually, I wadded up the paper sack and said, "Mike, time for me to go. If you want to stay up here, you can. But I have to start back."

I made a project of retying my boot laces to let him think it over, and then got up to set off down the trail. Mike arose, too, and as we began the descent he stayed right with me, picking his way down the rocky terrain. When we reached the lemon orchard, I pulled up and asked him if he wanted a lemon. Shaking his head, he said, "Nuh," and we continued on down the trail, through the fence, and up to the cottage. I unlocked the door and held it as Mike squeezed in and headed for his room.

"See you tomorrow, buddy," I said.

Chuck and Jody, along with several others, were waiting for me at the nursing station, brimming with questions. It turned out that about twenty minutes after I left, Jody had opened the door for a group of children returning from the food service building. In the midst of the rush Mike had darted out, and Jody had had to catch herself from calling him back as she saw him tearing off for the fence.

There was quiet satisfaction all around now, and when I stopped at Mike's room as I was leaving, there was another upbeat moment when he answered my question about what he wanted to do the next day.

"Hike up Dogfahs tumawah."

After collecting Mike the next day, we stopped at the school to draw. I was anxious to see what, if anything, his pictures would reveal of the last several weeks. He set to work at once and soon, without any prompting, he produced two drawings. The first he identified as a "twee."

It was a picture he had drawn before, but this time, significantly, there were no people. Ground and horizon lines ran across the page, tightly enclosing the landscape, meager as it was—barren limbs and a branchlike network that looked like bars. No leaves. I guessed that this was representative of Mike's regression, his attempts to reduce his world to a manageable level. And that meant keeping it simple, and without people.

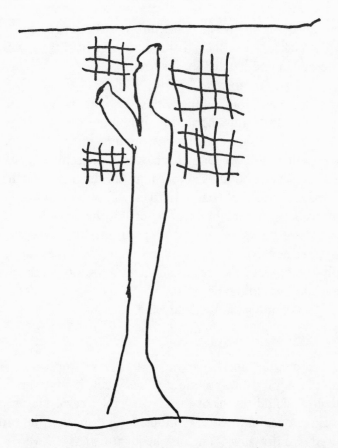

The next drawing was his conventional cottage scene. But again, there were no people outside, just one solitary stick person in the window whom I took to be Mike. The tiny figure was disproportionate to the size of the building, perhaps indicating that, once again, Mike saw himself as powerless, easily overwhelmed by outside forces beyond his control. And perhaps it was also significant that—as Mike so often did—the person was observing the world from the relative safety of his cottage.

I didn't question him, because the pictures told me all that was going to be expressed—I was hanging onto Mike's psyche by my fingertips.

I played it cozy for the next month, letting Mike set the tone. Gradually, he resumed his participation in school and became more communicative with the cottage staff. And we took up our twice-weekly hikes again, with Mike taking my hand for an occasional pull up and, in turn, helping me when I asked. Finally, some two and a half months after his father's appearance, Mike seemed to reveal, by his drawing of the two of us hiking on Dogface, that he was back to where he was before his father's visit.

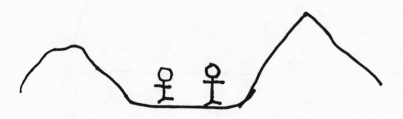

I studied the picture a moment. Mike, unaccustomed to not receiving an immediate "Good," looked up and met my eyes.

"That's a really nice picture, Mike . . . I'm so glad to see us hiking together again. . . . "

I let out a big sigh in Scott's office. "Well, we've turned the corner. But it was a close call."

"Yes, it was," Scott agreed. "And not just for Mike. There were moments back there when I thought you were going to bring in the Irish Mafia and put out a contract on Mike's dad."

"Yeh. I was resentful, frustrated—and angry. But I learned a lot. I just wish the exercise hadn't been at Mike's expense."

"But Mike bounced back," Scott retorted. "That's the important thing. And it also points up something else."

"What's that?"

"That Mike *can* bounce back, can cope. You're not the only one who learned something—Mike learned a lot about *himself* during that little interlude. He's got strengths that he didn't even know he had, and he was able to draw on them. He also discovered that there's somebody he trusts. And that, my young colleague, dictates the next step."

"Play therapy."

"Right. It should tell us whether Mike can move up another notch or two."

CHAPTER THIRTEEN

THE ROOM WE USED FOR PLAY THERAPY AT MERRICK looked more like a recycled laundry room than quarters for doing psychotherapy. A light green tiled floor with the tiles continuing halfway up the wall made for easy cleanup and an occasional hosing down; a shallow sink was in one corner and next to it was a sturdy wooden cabinet filled with a variety of toys and games. There were latex hand puppets, some of which resembled a family—including grandparents, a father, mother, brothers, and sisters—plus a fierce alligator, a one-eyed wolf, a friendly but unidentifiable mutt, and a dragon with a well-chewed tail. Also available were building blocks, simple wooden toys, checkerboards, watercolor paints and crayons, modeling clay, cap pistols, and a decommissioned beebee gun.

In one corner was a small sandbox, and to the side stood a four-foot plastic Bobo clown that was stuffed with foam rubber. His feet were weighted, and thus he always managed to regain them, and his dignity, no matter how malevolent the assault. His head was cocked where it had been taped back on after countless decapitations, which gave him an understandably perplexed look, and here and there spongy rubber protruded. But no matter how often he was bombarded and mutilated, his cheerfully composed features remained the same. Which was not always the case with the therapist.

To one side of a long, low table was an easel with sheets of shiny paper ready for drawing or finger painting, and to the left was the one-way window that looked like a mirror from inside the play area. It was covered with a wire screen that had numerous and sundry dents, but the window itself had somehow survived, although traces of paint and a few globs of clay had penetrated the screen. Children liked to make faces and grimace into the mirror, little realizing that there was often an observer on the other side making notes, or recording the proceedings on videotape for later study and evaluation.

Children's play is often viewed as frivolous, wasted time, an activity that is uncomplicated, lacking in direction, and simply a fringe benefit of childhood to be enjoyed before the oars of responsibility are lowered. To someone casually watching a group of children it may appear that way, but in actuality, play is vitally important to a child's development. In fact, an inability to mix and play with other children or by oneself is often an important symptom.

In play children not only express themselves but also learn about social interactions—getting along with others, rehearsing the fine points of asserting oneself, channeling aggression through competition, and of particular importance, providing the first linking up with members of the opposite sex. Play is far more complex than we imply by the phrase "child's play."

There is another equally significant dimension of play. When confronted by bewildering notions, worrisome or frightening feelings, or explosively hostile impulses, the young child senses that fantasy play is the safest way to release them. The greatest advantage is that the youngster is in control. If monsters get too scary, they can be dismissed with a mere shift of attention. Frustration and anger can be dissipated with a stern monologue accompanied by the crashing of toys.

On one occasion at the university clinic, I'd had a play therapy session with a four-year-old boy who carefully piled blocks one on top of another until he had built an elaborate tower. As he added the last block the tower began to sway, and abruptly the peaceful activity was transformed into a destructive tirade. Kicking and scattering the blocks around the room, he sternly addressed them: "Naughty blocks! Naughty, naughty, NAUGHTY! Don't you ever do that again or I'll send you to your room. Without supper! You won't have supper for a week! *Do you hear me?!*" His tone carried a strong parental inflection. Then, seemingly satisfied, he gathered up the errant blocks and quietly, painstakingly, began to rebuild.

Since play is one of the most important ways in which children declare themselves, it is that ongoing declaration that play therapy attempts to build upon, by setting up special conditions for the disturbed child. Oftentimes the youngster's choice of toys—what he does with them or has them say during play—reveals deep-seated conflicts, frightening fantasies, and occasionally, traumatic experiences. Thus, the antagonistic forces such as beset the child with his blocks are acted out and dispersed.

But first and foremost, play therapy is freedom. Freedom to explore, to test, to express feelings without fear of judgments being rendered or directions being dictated. And in this freedom the child, with the support of the therapist, has the opportunity to gain confidence in his or her own judgment of the way things are—and how one might go about changing what needs to be changed, or accept what can't be changed. Hence, the young child learns to work through the maze of negative emotions toward the parents—from ambivalence to fear, resentment, and anger. Later on, when others frustrate and anger him, this learning will carry over and the child will deal with the situation in ways that mirror a growing maturity.

It would be a real step up for Mike if he could participate in play therapy. The odds were against us, though. The severity of his disorder, the early onset, the apparent total lack of play in his life experience, all bespoke a poor prognosis. Still, Mike had improved significantly and this would be one way to find out just how far he could go.

I had begun preparing Mike for the shifts in treatment strategy just before our second Thanksgiving, wanting to give him enough time to make the adjustment. I brought it up first when we were seated on the summit of Dogface. He looked over at me quizzically when I mentioned that some new activities would be starting for him shortly. Two weeks later, just after his tenth birthday, we started play therapy.

Mike was already familiar with the playroom; we had used it now and then to escape inclement weather and still have somewhere to ourselves to draw some pictures or leaf through magazines. What had struck me was the fact that he had never shown the slightest interest in the toys in the

room. But that, I hoped, was more a consequence of his pre-
occupation than an indication of his inability to engage in
healthy fantasy and play.

Scott, who had agreed to observe these crucial first sessions, was already in the adjacent observation room when
Mike and I entered the playroom. Pulling up one of the
child-sized chairs, I gingerly seated myself; with my knees in
my line of vision, I always felt like a squatting Indian. Once
again, I went over what we would be doing.

"Mike, this is where we'll be coming twice a week.
You've been doing very well and now I want to try some new
things to see if they can help you even more. But we'll still go
on our hikes. Can't miss those, can we?"

An emphatic shake of the head.

"Right, but what we're going to be doing in here is playing—with the toys over there if you like, or painting a picture, or building things in the sandbox if you want. You can
play with anything in here, Mike." And then I paused, as I
remembered a time some months before when we had been
drawing pictures here. I had stepped out briefly and returned to find the water in the pint-sized sink running full-
blast and a mesmerized Mike regarding it with relish.

He had the same thought I did. He swiveled his head in
the direction of the sink.

I had to smile. "You remember the sink, I bet!"

"Mikoe wun waduh, go aw ovuh fwooah!!" came out
excitedly.

"That's right, we had a bit of mopping up to do, didn't
we?"

He nodded enthusiastically. He remembered well; the
sink had overflowed quickly, and by the time I returned
water was sloshing in torrential sheets over the sides. Fortu-

nately, the large drain in the middle of the floor had handled most of the deluge. Mike continued to nod vigorously, the pleasure of it all rekindled.

"Wun waduh . . . "

"Well, you can run the water again—but for using it in the sandbox over there, or for painting." And then, as gently as I could because I didn't want to establish any inhibitions, I added teasingly, "And no staring at the water . . . "

His head bobbed again, and he sneaked a last longing look at the beloved sink and faucet before surveying the room. But he wouldn't leave his chair. I sat watching him in silence for a while and then tried to encourage him to explore.

"There are a lot of toys in the cabinet, Mike. Remember, you can do anything you want in here. The toys are there for you to play with. And there's paper and crayons if you want to draw, and Bobo the clown over in the corner."

Mike got up slowly, paused, and then hesitated by the cabinet. I had opened the doors earlier and he bent over, cautiously scrutinizing the different toys. Then he moved on to the sandbox. But he only looked. He seemed very concerned about not touching anything.

He approached each part of the room this way—the painting easel, Bobo, the sink, even the mirror. Sometimes, after inspecting an object for a few moments, he would turn and look at me with a tentative expression. I wasn't sure if he was uncertain as to where to start first, or if he was having difficulty making the connection between the activity of play and the various objects. So each time he turned I smiled and nodded. He would watch me, seemingly trying to read something in my expression, and then resume his circuit. After twenty minutes or so of this, I realized that it was simply going to take time for Mike to feel comfortable enough to initiate anything resembling play.

Again I reassured him that this was his hour and he could spend it any way he chose, and by the end of our forty-five-minute session, it seemed as if Mike had done about three hundred laps around the room. I was almost dizzy, but I had also stayed patient and supportive, visualizing Scott's reaction in the observation room as he watched "Quick Results McGarry" exercise a little self-control.

Later, Scott complimented me on my forbearance. He also said that he hadn't really expected anything much different from how Mike behaved. Any real spontaneity would have been highly unusual.

The next two sessions were simply repeats of the first, with Mike continuing his tentative explorations around the room. On a few of his revolutions he would reach out slowly and touch Bobo the Clown, or place his hand hesitantly on the cool sand before quickly looking at me, his expression revealing wonderment. But the child's atavistic curiosity seemed to be consistently overridden by some urgent restraint.

For my part, it was difficult to sit quietly, awaiting Mike's first move. But in play therapy it is crucial that the therapist not direct, but rather allow spontaneous, uninhibited play. It is only in such an atmosphere that the child will feel assured enough to begin translating conflict into activity.

"It's hard to choose just what to play with first, isn't it?" I offered several times. But Mike would just glance blandly over and then continue his scrutiny.

In between sessions like this, we took our regular hikes on Dogface and then Mike was his usual inquisitive self, for that was a level of functioning that he had mastered. Finally, after the third meeting, Scott suggested I put paper and crayons on the table, articles Mike was comfortable with, and suggest that he draw if he wished.

I did so at the next session. Mike paced about the room for a bit and then came over and sat down by the crayons and paper. During the next few minutes he concentrated on his pictures. Mike seemed content to draw something and show it to me. Then we would examine the familiar scenes together. He was simply unable to make any exploratory gambits on his own.

Halfway through, I decided to provide more direction. This had gone on long enough. So, while he watched, I mixed paints and set them up in front of the easel; I took out the clay and molded a few crude animal shapes, leaving the rest on the table; I piled some of the blocks into a small arch and pushed a toy car through the opening. I even gave Bobo a couple of bops and Mike was entranced as the clown bounced up again.

"These are all things you can do too, Mike. You can play with any of the toys in here, do anything you want— paint, build blocks, play with Bobo, whatever . . . "

Mike inched over to where I was leaning against the toy cabinet.

"Wha' this?" he asked, picking up a soft, well-worn object with a red checkered shirt.

"A doll, Mike. Raggedy Andy is his name . . . "

Mike laid it gently back on the counter and picked up a small piece of pink modeling clay. He rolled it into a little ball and held it between his fingers while he passed it under his nose. I restrained myself from saying anything when his tongue flicked out and tasted it. At last, the examination complete, he laid the clay back down on the table. Taking several steps away from me, he reached his hand out toward the rubber dragon, then paused, withdrew it, and retreated back near me.

Mike just wasn't catching on and Scott and I spent considerable time discussing what to do about it. Finally, Scott backed my decision to become even more active. More and more I was coming to feel that I was going to have to teach Mike how to play. If that were possible.

I started our next session with the hand puppets, placing one on each hand and carrying on a conversation between them in which they expressed the hope that Mike would play with them. He watched attentively as the alligator and the dog discussed the situation, looking from one to the other as each said something, and then at me. He seemed intrigued, so I handed the mutt to Mike, showing him how to slip it over his hand. Then the alligator began talking again.

"Hi, Dog!" The alligator bobbed his head, but the dog remained motionless and silent.

"Hey Dog, I said 'hi'! Can't you say 'hi' back to me? Hi there."

But Mike was struck dumb.

I persisted. "Dog, what's your name?"

No response.

The alligator tried again. "Oh, I bet I know where you're from. You live on Dogface, that mountain out in back where Mike and Pat like to climb. Right?"

Mike looked up at me, pleased with the recognition of his favorite spot.

"Hey Dog, talk to me. Are you from Dogface?"

But no matter how I coached Mike, he couldn't make the transition from himself to playing a hand-puppet character.

"Well," concluded the alligator at last, "you don't have much to say, do you? I'm getting hoarse, doing all the talking. Just shake your head 'no' so I'll at least know you heard me!"

Mike sat looking at the dog, waiting patiently for it to shake its head. Finally, I reached over and rotated his wrist and the dog's head moved.

"Now *that's better!*" cheered the alligator.

Not much, I thought. Scott agreed with me.

CHAPTER FOURTEEN

THE CHRISTMAS HOLIDAYS ALWAYS BROUGHT ABOUT A magical transformation within the children's cottages. Instead of the usual institutional pallor, doors, walls and even the ceilings were trimmed in shiny tinsel and red and green crepe paper. Christmas carols played bravely through the static of the speaker system and sprigs of holly and berries added touches of color here and there. In Mike's cottage, a tall artificial Christmas tree stood near the nursing station, where its ornaments and lights could be properly supervised. And brightly wrapped presents cascaded from under the shimmering tree. Some of the kids didn't respond at all to the sudden change in the cottage surroundings and routine; they wandered about as if sleepwalking and, perhaps, ventured to taste the plastic poinsettias. But others became increasingly euphoric with each passing day.

The day before Christmas, school was canceled and shortly after noon the exuberant children were escorted to the dining hall, where they hastily gulped their sandwiches. Before long, the room was abuzz with anticipation. Then suddenly sleigh bells jingled from the adjoining corridor as Santa Claus arrived. A naturally overstuffed psychiatric aide savored the yearly role. Within minutes he had the youngsters singing Christmas carols. Most of the kids hummed off-key and mouthed their own lyrics, while the rest stared out remotely. Staff members circulated throughout the room, gently trying to involve the more disturbed children in the festivities.

As I moved among the youngsters myself, I would occasionally catch Mike's roving eye. He had never learned Christmas carols, of course, and now he seemed fidgety and uncomfortable. I realized with a twinge of sadness that, as with so many children here, Santa Claus and Christmas didn't mean a thing to him. But at least he was here; last year he had stayed in his room. . . . Finally, I went over and sat beside him.

"Isn't this fun, Mike? Having Santa here and eating cookies and ice cream?"

Mike looked up from the second helping of ice cream that he had just polished off, searching for more. Quite a bit of it had missed his mouth. "Mo' chok-let, Paht." He pushed the bowl at me.

"Enough ice cream for now, Mike." I took a napkin and, wetting it, tried to scrub some of the chocolate remnants from his face, while he squirmed away. Then, putting my hands on his shoulders, I pivoted him toward the center of the room, where some of the kids had clustered around Santa. "Watch now, Santa Claus is going to be handing out presents pretty soon. See, he's picking up his bag now."

Mike glanced about listlessly as Santa began moving up and down the aisles between the tables, dispensing multicolored packages. Sounds of ripping and tearing followed in his wake, punctuated by staccato yelps of pleasure. Teachers, aides, and nurses continued to mingle with the youngsters, encouraging the less able to open their gifts, sometimes taking a child's inert hands and helping to untie the bow and part the paper. Finally, Santa worked his way down our aisle and spied Mike. He came closer.

"Well, well, here's a young man who certainly deserves a surprise today. I'm glad you came this year, Mike."

I could feel Mike's shoulders tense as Santa moved in, so I whispered in his ear, "It's all right, he just wants to give you a Christmas present. It's okay—I'm right here."

Slowly, Santa knelt down beside him. "Mike, I understand you've learned to draw pictures and even ask for things. My, my . . . that's very, *very* good, and here's a nice present for you!" Reaching into his sack, he withdrew a large package covered with smiling snowmen and reindeer. "Merry Christmas, Mike."

Mike hesitatingly took the gift from Santa's outstretched arms and turned slowly toward me. He was plainly confused by the whole transaction. He glanced uncertainly from me to the box and back toward Santa, who was continuing his turbulent journey down the aisle. Then Mike focused his attention on the bow, giving it a tentative poke. When nothing happened, he eyed it suspiciously.

"Go ahead, open it. See what's inside," I encouraged. "It's for you."

But Mike didn't understand and finally I had to show him how to work his way through the ribbon and paper. I pulled away the last of it to reveal the carton with a shiny red truck showing through the cellophane wrapping. Removing it carefully from the box, I handed it to him. He seemed captivated, turning it over and over, observing it in minute detail.

"Wow, that sure is a beautiful truck, isn't it, Mike? Santa must think you're someone pretty special!"

Mike still didn't fully comprehend what was going on, but he was unmistakably interested.

"Trahk?"

"Truck, Mike," I intoned the drawn-out sound. "A toy truck just like the big one that delivers food up to the unit here. Now you have a truck of your own to play with."

Just then another child cruised by, spotted the sleek new truck, and pounced, trying to grab it away. In a flash, Mike's arms surrounded it and he yanked back, covering it protectively.

"Trahk . . . " he whispered softly, verbally caressing his new treasure.

At last, after all the gifts had been distributed, Santa asked everyone to join him in singing "Silent Night." By this time most of the children were staring impatiently around the room, checking out what others had received and already, predictably, a few altercations had erupted. The kids were becoming increasingly restless after two hours in the dining hall. Santa gathered up his bag and waved himself out the door; in the ensuing commotion, the staff began separating the youngsters for the walk back to the cottages. Parents would be arriving soon.

Mike and I took the long way back to his cottage, and I could sense his uneasiness diminish as we left the party behind. I still hadn't heard a word from the Harrises so, for Mike, this Christmas would be like all the others. He would stay here. It was probably just as well.

The next couple of hours were hectic ones. The parking lot soon filled to overflowing as families arrived to pick up their kids. Paper bags stuffed with clothing and marked with each child's name were handed to the parents, along with small brown envelopes containing enough medication to cover the long weekend.

By late afternoon, a strangely unfamiliar silence had fallen over Cottage 4. I walked down the long corridor to Mike's room, carrying the Christmas present that I'd brought up earlier from my office. Tapping on the door, I asked, "Mike, can I come in?"

No answer.

Pushing against the door lightly, I stepped partially inside. Mike was sitting in his chair, holding the truck on his lap and gazing out the window. I wondered if he had been watching the tableau in the parking lot, seeing all the other kids leaving with their parents. But if he had been, there was no outward sign.

I moved over to the bed and sat down, placing the gift beside me. "Did you have a good time this afternoon at the Christmas party? And seeing Santa Claus?"

He nodded absently, still watching out the window. There was no one out there that I could see.

"And your truck? Are you happy with the present Santa brought you?"

Another slight nod. He was off somewhere in a different world again. Something elusive was going on inside, but all I could do was try to pull him back.

"Mike, look at me."

His head rotated cautiously in my direction, but his eyes remained glazed and remote.

"Mike, are you okay? What's wrong?"

Another blank stare.

"Hey, are you with me, buddy? Are you here in this world?"

The only response was some rapid blinking. I peered intently at the somber little boy, baffled by the sudden change in his behavior. What on earth was going on behind that inscrutable mask? Whatever it was, though, he evidently couldn't bring himself to express it.

"Mike, why don't you come over here and sit next to me? Okay?" I patted the bed.

Still, there was no response. Seeing him walled off again was eerie. He hadn't been like this since the crisis of his father's visit. All I could do was wait. At last, Mike wrapped an arm securely around his truck, got up slowly, and shuffled over to the edge of the bed. He had not yet noticed the present.

I put my hand on his shoulder and for some time we sat quietly in the semidarkness of the settling dusk and listened to faint strains of Christmas music.

"Are you sad, Mike?"

A slight stiffening of the shoulders.

"It's all right to be sad. It's part of living—hopefully, a small part. But sometimes things make you feel sad, and that can hurt. And when that happens, there's nothing wrong with getting help from other people. I'd like to help you, Mike. Will you let me?"

Mike sat rigid and immobile, immersed in his thoughts. Finally, after another stretched-out silence, he looked down at his new possession.

"Trahk," he murmured faintly. Wherever he had been, he seemed to have returned.

"Mike, it's almost Christmas and that's a time when

people share gifts with their friends. It's a way of saying thank you for being such a nice person and good friend. So I brought my best friend and hiking buddy a present." Moving the package closer to him, I asked, "Want to open it?"

Mike glanced up at me quizzically, as if he had just realized I was there. Then, falteringly, he reached out to touch the box, carefully running his hand over the top, feeling the design in the paper. Again he needed help and together we untied the rather incompetent bow I had managed to produce. Then we folded the paper back to expose a black-and-white-checkered carton, but this time there was no hint as to its contents. Taking his hands in mine, we removed the lid and laid it beside the box, uncovering a layer of bright green tissue paper. Nudging it a couple of times, he seemed reluctant, almost afraid, to discover what lay beneath, until at last he pulled the paper away and peeked inside the box. His eyes got very big as he saw a pair of brand-new hiking boots and realized what they were meant to be used for.

"Hikin' boats . . . " he whispered.

"Merry Christmas, Mike." I could sense my own feelings surging up and I cleared my throat. "They may be a bit big for you now. You may have to wear a couple pairs of socks at first, but the way you're growing, they should fit you in no time. Like to try them on?"

Mike still appeared somewhat dazed, his eyes like saucers, but he nodded a vigorous "Yes!" Seating himself hastily on the floor, he yanked off his old worn-out boots and pulled on the stiff new ones. Without even bothering to lace them up tight, he stomped around the room, all at once happy as a clam with something he finally understood. On his fiftieth orbit, he halted abruptly by the door, puffing as he stood poised in mid-step.

"Shall we go show Chuck your new boots, Mike?"

He nodded eagerly. "Yes! Show Chahk!" he said. Picking up his truck, he bounded out into the hall and down to the nursing station, where he received many compliments on his new "boats" and his "trahk." I smiled when I saw Jody loading the truck with Christmas cookies for him.

But it soon became apparent that all the excitement and activities of the afternoon had left Mike exhausted. I sent him back to his room to put on his pajamas.

As he stared after the retreating figure, Chuck said, "You know, this is the first time Mike's ever really reacted to Christmas . . . at all. Before, he's always just withdrawn and avoided everybody." He shook his head. "Imagine, ten years old, and just experiencing his first Christmas . . ."

CHAPTER FIFTEEN

I HAD BEEN AT MERRICK FOR A YEAR AND A HALF NOW. My dissertation was going well and I hoped to finish it and receive my doctorate during the summer. I was amazed at how fast the time had gone, but nothing brought that home to me more than how Mike was shooting up and stretching out. There was usually a gap of leg between the hiking boot top and the cuff of his pants, and it seemed that at least once a month we had to go down to the Clothes Corner to pick out some bigger blue jeans or a larger shirt.

His speech had greatly improved, too. Once Mike began to attempt verbal communication, I couldn't believe how rapidly he put words together. Although he hadn't spoken intelligibly for several years, he must have had a good grasp of language before he sealed over. Now, after slightly more than a year of talking, much of his pronunciation, though not all, approximated normal speech. Perhaps the distortion was simply garbling that had occurred when Mike had internalized his language and shut out any feedback from others. But now he proved yet again that he was certainly not retarded—though I had never had any doubts about that. Once he became more receptive, he learned quickly, which was fortunate. We had no speech therapists at Merrick, so we usually just improvised.

Mike's dramatic improvement had created a ground swell of interest on the unit, and for some time now we had been planning similarly structured programs for some of the other youngsters. I sat in on these sessions as a consultant, gratified that I had made a contribution. Through sheer serendipity, of course.

After one such meeting, Chuck came over and we got to talking about Mike. "You know," he confided, shaking his head, "in all honesty I've got to admit it—I never thought you'd get *anywhere* with him. But it's incredible how much he's changed, and continues to change!"

It was nice to hear the admiration in Chuck's voice, but it also embarrassed me. "There wasn't any secret formula. Just a lot of luck," I shrugged. "Scott, of course, kept me hanging in there. He set me up, to begin with, by getting me so intrigued with Mike that I had to give it a try. And then he played my stubborn streak beautifully. Wouldn't let me quit. And you guys all encouraged me to stick with Mike, too."

"Yeah, but like I say, I never expected you to actually *get* anywhere with him! And I don't think too many others did, either. But he's really kicking up his heels. He identifies with you, imitates how you walk. And today, would you believe, I caught him saying, 'dammit'!"

"You're kidding. I can't imagine where he could have learned that—"

"Me neither." Chuck grinned. "But this morning I was going by his room and I heard a loud 'dommit.' Took a moment to register, so I stuck my head in the door and there's Mike, struggling with his jacket zipper. It was caught and he was yanking on it. Evidently he just got so frustrated he had to let it out, but he looked a bit sheepish when he realized I'd heard him. I told him it was okay, though—reinforced it, as you say—and said it was better for him to do that than hold it inside." Chuck paused and laughed. "It just about cracked me up on the spot, though, hearing him swear like that!"

Chuck's comments corroborated my own observations that Mike did seem to be moving into a new developmental phase. I had first noticed it a week before. We had just left the cottage for a play therapy session and were headed down the walkway when Billy, whose room was next to Mike's, came wheeling around the corner on a bike and yelled, "Hi!"

"Hi, Bil-*ee*," came right back from Mike and even Billy looked back over his shoulder in astonishment. It was the first time Mike had ever greeted him. Or, as far as I knew, any of the other children. And he had called him by name.

I stopped and stared at Mike while the impact of that spontaneous reply sank in. "Hey, that was really neat of you to say 'hi' to Billy like that. I'm proud of you!"

Mike was self-consciously studying the pavement, so I didn't press it, just gave him a squeeze on the back of the neck and left my arm resting lightly on his shoulder as we continued on down to the administration building.

Then, a couple of days after that incident, I saw Mike with Danny, the youngster who was so obsessed with his mathematical formulas and repetitious numbers. We hadn't had any success with Danny, but seeing the two boys together made me pause. Mike was intently studying the sheaf of papers Danny always pulled out. Then he said something, Danny pocketed his notes, and they both walked off in the direction of the riverbed.

Scott and I were talking in his office the next day when I glanced out the window and saw Mike and Danny together again. I called it to Scott's attention and we both got up and watched. Danny was evidently having one of his rougher days; he seemed to be hallucinating, stopping every few yards and speaking up into the empty sky. Mike kept urging him along the walk, retrieved him twice when he began wandering away, and refused to be put off by the bizarre behavior. Scott made a note to ask Conable about checking Danny's meds.

"Can't seem to get Danny stabilized. But look at Mike —boy, that's great to see. Do you know if he's relating to any of the other kids, Pat?"

"From what I hear, he is. It's interesting, Mike is usually with kids like himself—the sensitive, reticent ones. Kindred souls, I guess. He avoids those who probably bullied and teased him in the past. He must have had his own private accounting system during his noncommunicative years, and now he knows which kids he wants for friends."

"What about the staff? Anybody else noticing any changes?"

"Pretty much everyone at the cottage has reported the same. Chuck and Jody both say he's relating well to the nursing staff."

"Well, that sounds great. But still nothing much going on in play therapy?"

"No. It's been almost two months now, but Mike just can't initiate much activity on his own. I'm trying to encourage him, but haven't been very successful. Why don't you observe again soon, see what you think. I need a second opinion."

"Okay. It's hard to know if he's just not ready for it yet, or if he can't do it. Maybe it's going to be beyond his capabilities, Pat. You'd better start preparing yourself for that eventuality."

"Yeh, I know, Scott. I know, I know . . . "

Scott's glance was perceptive. "Back off a bit, remember?"

I saluted. "Aye, aye, Captain."

Later that afternoon when Mike and I were in the play therapy room, I told him what Scott and I had observed earlier.

"We saw you and Danny today, Mike. You were really helping him, and being very thoughtful and considerate."

Mike, embarrassed by my compliment, hunched down so I had to bend over to see his face.

"Thoughtful and considerate—do you know what those words mean?"

Mike shook his head and continued to avoid my eyes.

"Well, that means you're being a good friend to Danny. You spend time with him, watch out for him when he's having problems, don't let him wander off by himself. That's what friends do for each other—help each other when they need it. That's why I said you're being such a good friend to Danny. And that means you must like him and feel for him and care what happens to him. How does that make you feel?"

"I few good."

"Great, Mike. That's exactly what should happen. You know, when you do something nice for someone else, then you feel good about yourself, too."

Mike looked up at me. Then he said, as if it were so obvious that it hardly needed mentioning, "He my friend, I tichin' him ta hike, ahn' climb, ahn' name trees. About workin' togethuh, hikin'.."

"Good. Working together is very important—we've learned that, haven't we? And sharing, being friends. Like we are, like you and Danny, Chuck and Jody, and Cecile, too."

Mike was twitching, eager to begin drawing.

"You like Chuck and Jody a lot, don't you?"

He nodded self-consciously.

"That's okay, Mike. They're both very nice people who care about you, just as I do. Those are the nice feelings we have about someone who is very special to us. That's why we say that we love people when we care a great deal for them. When we want to share things with them, feel pleasure when we're with them, and sometimes feel lonesome when we're away from them."

Mike had taken a crayon and was idly twisting it in his fingers, pulling at the paper covering.

"You know, not everyone can share his feelings with others, Mike. So that makes you someone very special. Because you give, and you don't hold back anymore when you want to do something to help someone else. Many of us here—Jody, Chuck, me—we care a great deal about you, even love you. Did you know that?"

Mike's head snapped up and he stared at me, open-mouthed. "You *wuv* me?"

"Yes, I love you, Mike. And it's a very special kind of love, because I'm a doctor who cares very much about you, and wants to see you get much better. Just as Jody and Chuck do—all the staff people, really. They love you, too. Does that surprise you?"

Mike nodded, again self-conscious. This was all rather confusing for him. Not the easiest thing in the world to understand—or explain, for that matter.

"What I'm trying to say, Mike, is that you're going to feel good when you care for people, when you help someone like Danny, because he's your friend. And you're going to love people, too, and care about what happens to them. I want you to know how proud I am of what a good friend you are, sharing your feelings with others and doing nice things for them to make them feel good and, more important, make you feel good, too."

Mike was sitting very still; he'd dropped the crayon in his lap and was staring at his hands.

"I guess in all fairness, though, Mike, we should also talk about the fact that sometimes things will happen that hurt, make you feel bad. We may do something and feel sorry about it later, or somebody may say something that hurts us, makes us feel bad inside. Like when your dad came that day. But if we learn to understand what we're feeling, to know that the hurt will go away, then it becomes a little easier to take."

Mike seemed to be memorizing the lines on his hands. This was a tough area, especially for him. But it was one that needed to be dealt with. For Mike, handling his feelings was going to involve a great deal of new learning and other accompanying adjustments. So much of what he had previously acquired had been covered with a shroud of fear. And there were still so many experiences and emotions that remained unknown to him.

But there was no doubt about it. More and more Mike was asking questions about what went on around him, and usually spontaneously. On one occasion when we saw a recently admitted child having a temper outburst, Mike showed a marked curiosity. I explained about anger, reminding him of times when he had felt frustrated, and how that led to feelings of anger and the actions—like stomping off—that he had taken.

Another time we came upon a young girl sobbing uncontrollably and, after comforting her and finding a psychiatric aide to help her back to her cottage, we talked about it. When Mike asked, "Why she cry?" it meant everything from what does crying mean—how is it possible for someone to cry both when he's happy and when he's sad—to how does a person cry, or stop crying? I tried to help him grasp the concept of emotional expression by interpreting what we observed and helping him to identify his own feelings.

In this context, we often talked about physical affection and how it was demonstrated by holding hands, hugging, and kissing. The nature of his questions indicated that some serious reasoning was taking place. Mike could not remember anyone ever expressing affection to him; until relatively recently, he hadn't given anyone much of a chance to. So he was very uncertain about hugs and kisses. But holding hands seemed to be okay, and with increasing frequency he began to take mine. Soon he was doing it automatically. Wherever we went—to the farm, the water tanks or filtration plant, the canteen, even up into the hills—we held hands. There seemed to be basic reassurance and stability in that very simple act.

But giving a person a hug seemed unsettling and scary to him, and not something he could initiate himself. Mike had his ways, usually very subtle, of conveying when something was beyond his reach. I had sensed this constraint and so, one day as we were lacing up our boots for another assault on Dogface, I proposed a new requirement:

"Mike, before we take off today, I'd like to give you a

big hug and I'd like you to give me a big hug back. Would you do that for me?"

Mike looked up sharply, then bent back down to adjust the laces of his hiking boots.

"Mike?"

He was scared, but moved slowly in front of me, eyes averted.

"One big hug for each other, then we'll be off for Dogface."

I leaned over and put my arms around him, giving him a squeeze. Tentatively, his arms went around my neck, but he remained stiff and uncertain.

"Good, Mike. That's a great start. Wasn't so bad after all, was it?"

Mike shook his head mutely; he still couldn't bring himself to look at me.

"Okay?" I said, reaching for his hand. "Ready for Dogface?"

Mike raised his head, squinting in the direction of his favorite spot, and said, "Yes, we go hike Dogfahs."

From then on I required Mike to give me a hug each time I came to get him and whenever we parted. Gradually, he relaxed and allowed himself to enjoy the physical contact and affection. And in time, he even began to hug first, without being asked. Still, although touching and the burgeoning friendships were signs of significant growth, the underlying psychological situation was more mixed. There continued to be very little emotional expression. Despite the happiness I could sense just beneath the surface, Mike had yet to laugh spontaneously, or get overtly angry, or cry. These emotional outlets were still capped. Perhaps such feelings would come eventually; and then again, as Scott had warned me, there was the possibility that they might never emerge at all.

At times it seemed as if things were falling into place, but then a drawing would seem to indicate the opposite. I guessed that it was all part of Mike's working through the trauma of his early years. One afternoon he drew this rather austere picture of a house:

The severe, cold characterization depicted a formidable door, dark and out of proportion, with a large doorstop at its base. The three windows were tiny and devoid of curtains. At its worst, Mike's world seemed to be confined to that dreary institutional cottage. It *was* a very depressing place, I had to admit. Mike's choice of colors—deep purple and black—demonstrated that and, I presumed, accurately reflected his mood.

These occasional bleak periods seemed to be holding actions, providing Mike with an interval to consolidate his gains. But each time I held my breath, wondering if he had reached the level that would prove to be his developmental limit.

CHAPTER SIXTEEN

"We do somethin' diff'rent today."

"All right . . . " Such a statement was a new wrinkle, and I was somewhat taken aback. "What would you like to do, Mike?"

Without answering, he marched purposefully to the toy cabinet. I could feel my neck tingling as he reached inside, drew out the hand puppets, and carefully lined them up in a row on the table. He poked at the rubber faces, watching each sink in and then pop out when he released his finger. Mike seemed to be talking under his breath; then he broke off to share his conclusions.

"This dahdee, this mommy, this girl, this babee, this dog, this—" and he stopped, looking puzzled.

"That's a dragon, Mike," I offered.

"This drah-gun," he finished, and turned to see my reaction.

"Very good, Mike, you named all of them. That's very, very good!"

He gave an emphatic nod and spent the remainder of

the session pulling toys out of the cabinet and asking what they were. When we were through, I gazed about the cluttered room. Everything that could possibly have been extracted from the cabinet lay strewn about everywhere. As Mike reexamined first one object and then another, naming each of them again, I felt nothing but gratitude for the mess.

We were back the next day. Mike went immediately to the cupboard and gathered up several toys. He had brought his truck with him this time and, climbing into the sandbox, he proceeded to push it and a train caboose through the sand. I had asked Scott to observe again today and, although I couldn't see him, I smiled through the one-way mirror. I knew he'd be enjoying this new development as much as I was.

For the next several weeks, Mike actively played with many of the toys. I encouraged him to explore freely, and once again, I was amazed by the speed with which he grasped ideas. The pattern that evolved was interesting to follow. Mike was like a shopper, tentatively testing the watercolors until he felt at ease, then moving on to clay, then more toys, and finally games. He was particularly taken with the wire slinky, which he "walked" down a series of wooden boxes. He would become totally absorbed as the wire spring wiggled and jiggled down the "steps," quickly making adjustments in the position of the boxes whenever the slithering toy altered course.

The hour of play went too fast as far as he was concerned, and I began to get a plaintive, "Stay a liduh longuh, Paht? Please, Paht . . . jus' a liduh longuh?"

How could anyone say no to that? I certainly couldn't.

Mike's momentum was building. One afternoon when we were scheduled to hike on Dogface, he asked if we could

go to the playroom to draw instead. Again I was surprised.
Usually he dashed off his pictures in the dayroom or outside
under a tree. I went along with him, wondering why he was
postponing his hike; it wasn't like him. When we got to the
playroom, he quickly collected some paper and the crayons.

"All set? Ready to draw your pictures, Mike?"

He nodded, working busily. He was quietly occupied
for some time and I was absently pushing some modeling
clay when I became aware that Mike was standing next to
me.

"Hi, Monkey's Uncle. What's up—you got something
for me?"

He nodded shyly, looking down at the floor as he
handed me a piece of paper. I scanned it thoughtfully,
feeling a surge of elation as I realized what it conveyed:

Two hikers stood together on Dogface, hand in hand,
each one smiling broadly . . .

I couldn't believe it. Finally, after literally hundreds of
drawings of people without faces, here were two individuals
who were *not* looking the other way! The figures were still
crude, the features consisting merely of dots for eyes and
nose and a curved line for a smile—*but the faces were there!*
And the figures were holding hands!

"Mike—" I began, and then my throat caught and all I
could do was look at him and shake my head. "That super
picture deserves a big hug, don't you think?"

Mike smiled bashfully—actually *smiled!* His first real
smile! And yelped a little when I squeezed too tight.

"That's really a great picture, Mike. This must be you
here, right?" I pointed to the figure with the bigger grin.
"And this is me—the one with the big head? We look pretty
happy, don't we?"

Mike nodded self-consciously, squirming slightly as I continued to admire his drawing.

"Do you suppose you could draw another picture just like this one for me to keep? I know you'll want to put this one above your bed, but I'd sure like to have one of my own. What do you think—would you do that for me?"

His head bobbed agreeably and he bounded back to the table, grabbing a crayon to begin another masterpiece.

Later that afternoon I recounted the incident at the review meeting, and after the picture had been passed around and the chatter abated, I asked the team to be alert for more new developments. It turned out to be another significant stride. Soon reports were coming in from aides and nurses that Mike was becoming more sociable, acknowledging more people, calling everyone by name. He was even getting into a bit of mischief at school. Cecile laughingly told me that she had allowed Danny and Mike to sit together in class, but that she had had to gently reprimand them a number of times for goofing around.

"It was all I could do to keep a straight face, because actually I was just delighted to see them acting like a couple of normal cutups! And they're so good for each other. Both boys have started collecting rocks and cactuses and they're building a classroom garden together. It was their own idea. I couldn't be more pleased. In many ways, Mike's having far more success with Danny than any of us have!"

As Mike began to assume the lead, I was only too willing to relinquish it. Scott had been preparing me for this transition. Months ago he had told me, "With someone as deeply withdrawn and out of touch as Mike is, extraordinary measures are required. Sometimes when these individuals need to lean on you psychologically, you virtually move into their psychological space and take over. But once they're going under their own steam, the therapist has to sense at what point to begin stepping back, allowing the patient to resume control once again—at his or her own pace, of course. It's a slow, difficult process, but this is the time when the self theorists, with their commitment to providing psychological support and backing, are at their best.

"Watch Mike carefully. Give him the opportunity to test, to explore, to reach out. And expect to be amazed; kids can be so responsive and unpredictable. But remember, Mike's still a very, very disturbed youngster, and whether or not he can ever make up for all that lost time and trauma remains to be seen. Your responsibility is to take him as far as he can—and wants to—go. Okay?"

At the time I'd nodded, sobered by the consideration that it was, indeed, quite possible that complete recovery and discharge from the hospital might not be a part of Mike's future. But the thought of his having to spend his whole life at Merrick was so abhorrent that I quickly shoved it out of my mind.

That summer was marked by accomplishments for both Mike and me. I successfully defended my dissertation and was at last awarded my doctorate. I was relieved to have finished up, but after eight years of grinding study, the degree was almost an anticlimax. What I thoroughly savored, though, was the new title that preceded my name. Every time the paging system crackled, "Dr. McGarry, dial 296," I was inwardly thrilled—"Hey, that's *me!*"

And Mike kept progressing. He became noticeably bolder, willing to take chances and risks. Not long after Cecile reported the classroom misbehavior, Mike ventured into that great childhood pastime—testing the limits. It was mid-June, but already the weather was unbearably hot and sticky.

One Wednesday afternoon, Mike and I drove down to the canteen, forsaking our hike. The breeze through the open car windows provided only minor relief and we were both anticipating the air-conditioned snack bar. I slid my old Ford into a parking space next to a shiny new Cadillac, casually commenting on the disparity between the two vehicles. Mike looked over and then, apparently unimpressed, opened the door, bumping it against the side of the Cadillac.

I had started to get out, but paused when I heard the thud. "Be careful, Mike. Don't open the door into another car."

He sat there, holding the door, and a kind of impishness crossed his face. Then he pushed the door into the side of the car again, even harder this time.

"Mike—don't do that again!"

I had visions of an irate Cadillac owner bearing down on us, and the weather would definitely not be in our favor. Mike seemed to be measuring my resolve; then, rearing back swiftly, he subjected the Cadillac to another solid thump.

That did it. I reached across the seat, grabbing his arm and pulling him toward me.

"Mike, that's enough! I want you out of this car *right now,* and don't you touch that door again!"

Suddenly Mike was frightened; he knew he had gone too far. He was very subdued as he slid across the seat, climbed out, and slunk around the car, eyes focused on the ground.

A quick inspection revealed no damage to the Cadillac and also provided a few moments for me to consider how best to handle the incident. I closed Mike's door and then approached him, kneeling down so he would have to look at me. But before I could say anything, Mike said very softly, "Mik'l won't bahng the cah doah again—" His voice quavered; he was a very scared little boy.

"Mike—" I began, and then stopped as I saw that tears were beginning to stream down his cheeks. How long had it been since he had cried? Gently I put my arm around his shoulders and guided him to a nearby bench. He sat quietly, scrunched down, awaiting some kind of punishment.

"Mike, I want you to understand what just happened here. I was disappointed and irritated with what you did, but I also know why you did it. You wanted to see if I would still like you even if you were naughty and did something bad. You were really just testing me—and that's okay. But I also want you to know that if I get irritated or even angry with you, it doesn't mean I don't love you anymore, because I do. It just means that at the moment when you did something you weren't supposed to do—and *knew* you weren't supposed to do—I was angry. But I still love you and we can certainly talk about it, like we are now."

Mike watched me intently, listening carefully, and as I finished he was sobbing quietly. I put my arms around him and held him tightly as he buried his face in my shoulder, the accumulation of hurt and disappointment and fear pouring out. Perhaps, too, the tears expressed sheer disbelief that— at last—someone truly cared for him, no matter what he did. He was beginning to reach some of those agonizing, long-stifled feelings, and they were terrifying for him.

For some time after he stopped crying we sat and talked. Then, when I was certain he was feeling better, I gently led him back to the incident.

"Do you remember what you were thinking and feeling when I told you not to bang the door again, Mike?"

He looked thoughtful, a slight frown wrinkling his forehead. "I do' know. It jus' hahpen, the doah jus' hit the cah. Then I jus' did it again."

I believed him. It seemed like the kind of confronting,

impulsive behavior that pops out of children, with no rhyme or reason. Or, if there is some motive, it's buried.

"Then you saw me, your friend, getting angry. What did you feel then, do you remember?"

Again Mike thought, at last looking up at me. "Scahred?"

"Okay, what did scared feel like, Mike?"

"It hurt—heah—" and he rubbed his stomach, "ahn' heah—" Mike's hand clutched his chest. "I afwaid . . . ahn' scahred, few bahd aw ovuh."

"And unhappy?" I asked.

"Unhahppy, too." Mike looked dismal as he recalled it.

"All right, Mike, so unhappy is feeling bad, the opposite of happy, like when we do something fun and enjoy it. I'm sorry that you had to feel hurt and scared and unhappy. But it's good that you felt those feelings, knew what they were, and most important, shared them, talked about them with your friend. Do you know why that's good?"

He shook his head, picking at strings on a blue jean patch.

"How do you feel now?"

Again, the self-examination. "Okay."

"Do you know why you feel better now?"

"Nuh."

"Because you talked about the feelings, could tell me what they were and how they made you feel. So the unhappy or bad feelings have been let out by talking about them and not keeping them inside you. Now when something happens that makes you feel like that, you know what to do, don't you?"

"Talk!" Mike said emphatically.

This was another milestone and a particularly meaningful one. Scott cautioned me that the limit testing would more than likely recur; Mike needed to become better acquainted with his rebellious, misbehaving side. What it amounted to was more catch-up childhood behavior.

One afternoon Mike took me to the school and proudly showed me the rock garden he and Danny were building. Then, spotting some paper and crayons, he flopped down at his desk and began drawing. I was leafing through a large atlas when it struck me how quiet it was—*too* quiet. I looked up to see Mike standing next to a heavily crayoned wall, the scribbling hand dropping in mid-line as he became aware of my attention. He turned slowly, awaiting my reaction.

Saying nothing, I glanced at the sink where the soap and sponge lay. Mike followed my gaze, then proceeded to draw another few lines before again turning to watch me, a nervous twitch tugging at the corners of his mouth as he continued to push for a reaction.

Finally, when none was forthcoming, he sighed deeply and said, "Mik'l not draw on the wall. I few bahd, un-hahppy. Not do it again."

Then he walked over to the sink, wet the sponge and soap under the tap, and began to scrub the crayon marks off the wall. When he had finished, I asked him to come over and sit by me. He slumped down, repeating his earlier admonition to himself that he wouldn't draw on the wall again.

I spelled out for him the parallel between the car-door incident and drawing on the wall, once more reassuring Mike that we were still the best of friends, and that there was nothing he could do that would have an effect on how much I cared for him. I particularly stressed that things like this happened to all boys and girls as a part of growing up.

Mike listened solemnly.

"Okay, buddy, ready to go hiking now?"

He bounded out of his chair, the misbehavior immediately forgotten. I could only shake my head ruefully; he really was getting to be like other kids.

A couple of weeks later, Mike produced this picture after we had splashed around in the hospital pool. I interpreted it as an indication that Mike was still unsure of himself and of our relationship. He identified me as the one with the blank face.

Then, the following week, came a picture of us hiking on Dogface, the hues more vivid and varied as Mike expanded his repertoire from blues and browns to brighter, happier colors. And he had given me a smiling face again.

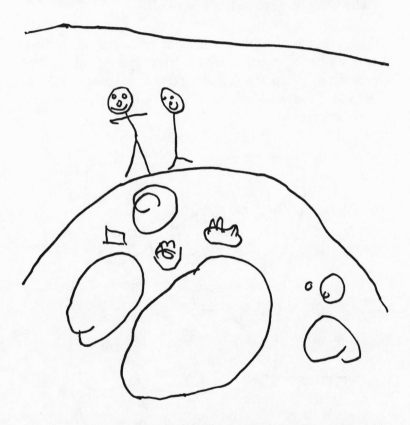

A few days after that, we were driving around the hospital grounds, content to enjoy the lovely day. Instigating our identification game, I pointed to a eucalyptus tree on the side of the road.

"What kind of tree, Mike?"

"Pep-puh—pep-puh tree," came back.

"Huh? C'mon, Mike, you know better than that. What's that one coming up?" There was a row of eucalyptus lining the roadway.

"Pep-puh—they all peppuh trees."

I pulled over to the edge of the pavement. This was an unexpected turn of events and I didn't know quite what to make of it. Mike had identified these same trees many times before.

"Hey, what's going on? You know a eucalyptus tree when you see one, Mike."

He was looking out the window, concealing his face from me. Suddenly there was a muffled snicker, then a cascade of giggling. He was actually laughing!

"I fuood you, Paht! I was tee-zun you . . . like you do to me . . . " and another spasm of chortling.

"Why you little—" I began, trying to appear very indignant at his tricking me. "You mean, you were just *teasing?* Well . . . " I huffed.

Gale-force giggles followed this. He was breaking himself up, and my pretended indignation really had him going. I reached over and gave him my affectionate neck squeeze.

"Okay, now we're even. You got me good!"

Later when I recorded the incident on his chart, I paused as the realization sank in: that was the first time that Mike had ever laughed out loud, teased, or played a joke. The Little Shadow was getting there . . .

That was the first time, but it certainly wasn't the last. Mike delighted in teasing me about the tree names, and my feigned indignation always broke him up—another game had evolved. Reports started to come back from the cottage, and the classroom too, that Mike was kidding around, laughing, and beginning to behave like a little kid.

Mike's sense of humor carried over into his drawings, too, and he began to present me with put-ons like upside-down faces, which he would hand me with great seriousness, and then snicker gleefully when my eyes widened at the absurdity.

Gasping and guffawing, he would confide, "Mik'l tee-zun Paht—put mouf on *top* head!!"

Such responsiveness built momentum, and soon I was prodding Mike to make his pictures more representational, more complex. Following my prompting for details like clothes, fingers, and shoes, he produced this drawing of the two of us at the water tanks. The runged ladders had made quite an impression.

One day he sneaked up behind me and tried to tickle me in the ribs. He was giggling and there was mischief in his eyes. So, unmercifully, I pulled the oldest trick in the book:

"Look out, Monkey—there's someone behind you. He's gonna get you . . . "

Mike spun around to look and in that instant I caught him, picked him up off the ground, and tickled the daylights out of him. He loved it, laughing and squealing and gasping for breath. Finally, though, Mike wore me down. I think he probably could have survived, even thrived on, several consecutive hours of tickling—after all, there were so many years to make up for.

From then on we spent a lot of time just horsing around. An odd kind of therapy perhaps, but as Scott had said, "If it works, do it!"

CHAPTER SEVENTEEN

WHEN I CALLED FOR MIKE A FEW DAYS LATER, HE CAUGHT me off guard again by not asking for a hike. Readily taking my hand, he accompanied me to the administrative cottage and, once in the playroom, followed his usual routine, inspecting the toys thoroughly before deciding which one he wanted. After twenty minutes or so, he settled down with the mother and father hand puppets. Some kind of involved conversation seemed to be going on, but his voice was so low that I could make out only an occasional word. Abruptly, Mike removed the puppets from his hands and laid them side by side on the table, staring at them pensively. Then he gave a deep, extended sigh. I watched him closely; something significant was happening.

"What are the mommy and daddy doing, Mike?" I asked.

A pause. "Sleepin' . . . "

"Sleeping, huh. Where are they sleeping?"

"Ah hoome . . . "

"Oh. Is it a nice home?"

"Uh huh."

"Are the mommy and daddy happy?"

"I do' know." Mike turned and looked at me. "Yes, hahppy."

"What's the mommy like, Mike?"

A shrug. "Do' know."

"And the daddy, do you know what he's like?"

Mike picked up the father puppet and studied it. "Dahdee nice."

He put it back down, and I thought, what a beautiful example of a child's capacity to forgive.

"So, it's a nice house and a nice daddy, but you're not too sure about the mommy? Would you like to know more about the mommy, Mike? Your mommy?"

Another shrug. He looked down, then murmured, "Yes."

"You haven't seen her in a long time, have you?"

Mike shook his head.

"And you miss her? Would you like to see her again?"

"Yes." A long silence. Then, his gaze still fastened on the puppets, he said, "Mik'l go un hoome bisit, Paht?"

"You'd like to see your mom and dad? And go on a home visit?"

A vigorous nod.

"Well, I can write to them. You know, though, that for a long time your mother wasn't well. Maybe she's better now. But Mike . . . "

"What?"

"Maybe it would be better if we ask them if they'd like to come and visit you here first. That way you could take them around, show them your room and all your drawings. Plus the cactus-rock garden that you and Danny made. That would be fun. Would that be okay?"

"Yes, thaht be okay. Then we go—"

"Then maybe after they've come here a few times, we could talk about a home visit."

"Okay."

The remainder of that session was spent talking about Mike's separation from his parents. I tried to tell him, in words he could understand, about the nature of severe emotional problems, putting my explanation in a context of withdrawal, not having any friends, and feeling bad all the time. And why it was sometimes necessary for a person to come to a hospital for care and treatment. Mike sat across from me, his chin cupped in his hands, and nodded from time to time. When I asked if he had any questions, he just shook his head and went over to the sandbox.

Later that afternoon, I wrote a letter to the Harrises telling them of Mike's request. Would they please call or write me at the earliest opportunity. I added a paragraph saying how much Mike had improved and that a visit at this point was particularly important to him. And, just for insurance, I stressed that since certain arrangements would have to be made for this meeting, they should let me know when they could come. I hadn't a clue whether they'd respond or not. If I didn't hear from them within a few weeks, I'd make another house call.

But a week later a hastily scrawled postcard arrived. The Harrises would like to see Mike, and they asked if I would call them. A number was at the bottom; Mr. Harris had finally relented and they now had a telephone. Before I left the hospital that day, I spoke briefly with Mrs. Harris, who sounded much better. As we were talking, her husband came home and she went outside to get him.

Mr. Harris wasn't used to the telephone. He shouted into it, and I had to hold the receiver at arm's length while we settled on a day. They would come the following Friday, meet with me for a while, and then spend some time with Mike.

"I'll see you at the administrative cottage at one o'clock, Mr. Harris," I concluded.

"One o'clock Saturday," yelled Mr. Harris. "See you then."

"Friday, Mr. Harris. One o'clock *Friday*. I'm not here Saturday." I caught myself shouting back at him, afraid he'd hang up.

"Oh, Friday you say? Right, see you then." Crash went the receiver in my ear.

When I told Mike about the impending visit, his response was immediate and unrestrained.

"Mommy, Dahdee come *here?!* Come see Mik'l?!" He began jumping around, waving his arms and chattering. "My dahdee ahn' mommy come see Mik'l. Come take Mik'l hoome. Cahn we hike Dogfahs now ahn' go to cahn-teen for ice creemcone? Paht? Okay, Paht?"

I smiled down at the barrage of questioning.

"Hey, take it easy. One question at a time, old buddy. This is just going to be a visit. They're not going to take you anywhere this time. But they want to come and see you, Mike, so they're coming on Friday. If we hurry now, we can sneak in an ice cream cone before my next appointment. Let's go."

Mike was so exuberant that I took the opportunity to raise another important matter. It was the umpteenth time I had broached the issue. "Mike, with both your mother and father coming to see you, wouldn't you like to look your best?"

A suspicious scowl—he knew instantly what I was getting at.

"Well, you do want to look nice for your mother, don't you, Mike? And there's nothing to worry about. I'll be right there, holding your hand. In fact, we could get haircuts together. And then we'd both be ready to meet your folks. Okay? How does that sound?"

It was a most difficult decision for Mike, but he finally acquiesced without enthusiasm.

"Paht, you be with Mik'l *all the time*—not let them *hurt* me?"

"I promise, Mike, I'll be with you—right beside you— the whole time. Nobody's going to hurt my hiking buddy."

The next morning I talked with one of the hospital barbers, thoroughly preparing him so as to avoid any mishaps. Then, a little while later, with Mike still vacillating, we went over to the barbershop together.

But once we arrived, there were no problems. Initially Mike was skittish, holding the mirror with one hand and me with the other. He watched the proceedings intently, but slowly a smile crept over his face as he relaxed and felt safer.

"How's that look, Mike?" asked the barber.

Mike carefully examined his hair, running his hand over the evened-out surfaces.

"It look nice!"

"What do you say to the barber, Mike?"

"Tonk you, Mista Bahbah, fuh haah-cut."

"You're welcome, Mike. Come see me again."

"Okay." He turned to me with alacrity. "Now you, Paht. *You* get haah-cut!"

As I climbed into the barber's chair for the institutional haircut I had had some second thoughts about, I reflected wryly that there was certainly nothing wrong with Mike's memory.

On Friday, the rusty Cadillac Fleetwood came pop-popping into the parking area a half-hour late. I escorted the Harrises directly to my office. I was reassured to see that both of them seemed fairly stable—Mr. Harris a bit more subdued and friendly, Mrs. Harris far more intact and alert.

But they were both rather uncomfortable and I spent some time making small talk—about the unseasonable weather, the coming election—in an attempt to put them at ease. Remembering Mrs. Harris's fear of the hospital, I was particularly concerned about her. I asked if they still went to the mental health center and Mrs. Harris was quick to nod yes, volunteering the information that she was regularly taking medication. The drug she mentioned was a well-known antipsychotic, and it was evident that it was doing its job. The hallucinations, the psychotic withdrawal had receded. Though still shy and reticent, Mrs. Harris was a different person from the woman I had met that day in Reidsville.

Finally I began filling them in on Mike's progress, stressing that he was relating much better, had some friends, could express affection, hold hands, hug—in short, that he had come a long way. And then I asked them about Mike's earlier years, explaining how little we know about schizophrenia and its development. Besides, I was curious about how they saw Mike's problems, and I wanted to hear their side of the story. I wondered how it would mesh with the original records.

"Can you recall how it all started?"

After several moments of silence, Mike's father sighed. "It was never easy. Michael was . . . always difficult. The slightest thing would upset him, 'specially if it was something different. Then he'd fuss. And whenever we wanted him to do something, he'd get *really* upset. Like, we'd ask him to pray with us. Instead, he'd throw the most unbelievable temper tantrums—worse than you could ever imagine. Lots worse than that time I came out here. . . . Or when I'd try to quiet him down or take something away from him—or even try to get him to play with one of his toys instead—he'd run away from me screaming and holding his hands over his ears. We knew there was something wrong, we just didn't know what to do . . . "

Mike's mother had been nodding from time to time as he spoke, and when he stopped, she haltingly began.

"Dr. McGarry, I've never mentioned this to anyone before—"she glanced nervously at her husband before continuing, "because Gerald has always felt so responsible. But I've always thought . . . well, that the problems started because of the hard time I had when Mikey was born and then all the sickness he had at the beginning. It was a very long labor—and he was a blue baby, too, and very tiny, weighed only four pounds. They had to keep him at the hospital for several weeks. . . . After he came home, he never slept, just cried and cried and cried. I couldn't take it. . . . I got sick, too. Pretty soon the doctor was coming to see both Mikey and me. He gave Mikey shots and I could tell how Mikey just *hated* them. And—as young as he was—I just *knew* that Mikey . . . hated *me* . . . blamed *me* for causing him all that . . . " Her voice caught and she shook her head morosely.

"I don't think Mike ever hated you, Mrs. Harris," I said, "or even blamed you. But it was certainly a tough way for him to be introduced to the world, wasn't it?"

Mrs. Harris was weeping, and her husband reached over and cradled her hand between his two ruddy ones. He looked at me. "The social worker at the mental health center said that we should ask you about Mike—whether you think we can take care of him if he comes for a home visit. We were also wondering . . . what will happen to him now that he's getting older."

"Well, that brings up some points we need to discuss. The serious mental problems he's had are in remission now. That means that he's not doing the things that were so distressing for you—throwing tantrums, lighting fires, running away. But there's no getting around the fact that Mike is way behind, and there's a very good chance that he'll always need some care and help. On the other hand, I don't believe that he'll have to spend the rest of his life in a hospital. I think it's quite possible that in time Mike could make a good adjustment to a group home.

"But what you'll have to prepare yourselves for at the moment is this: even though Mike is now ten years old, and he's really grown—he's quite tall for his age—his stature is misleading. His mind is more like a child of five or so. The severity of the schizophrenia has caused him to miss an awful lot, and whether he'll ever be able to make it all up is questionable. His psychological makeup is still rather fragile —much stronger than when you came up here last time, Mr. Harris—but Mike will always be an extremely sensitive person, very much attuned to how others behave toward him."

Mr. Harris averted his eyes, and I paused to let that sink in before going on.

"But Mike is also a very giving, loving person. He has a lot going for him, and a lot to share. He wants to spend time with his mother and father now. He's curious, sees all the other kids visited by their parents, going on home visits, doing things together. And he'd like to sample those experiences himself. Since Mike seems to be ready for this, I hope you folks will want to get to know your son again."

Both parents nodded agreeably, although Mrs. Harris still appeared somewhat apprehensive. I called the cottage to have Mike sent down, and then we talked a while longer as I answered more of their questions. At last Mrs. Harris's skepticism overcame her and she blurted,

"Is Mikey *really* doing that much better?"

"Well—" I began, but was interrupted by the familiar high-pitched voice wafting down the hall. "You'll see for yourself in about three seconds."

At that moment Mike burst through the door, his face flushed and jubilant.

"Dahdee, Mommy—I go for hoome bisit with you?"

I had to laugh at his directness. "Now wait a second, Mike," I cautioned. "How about sitting down for a few minutes and talking before you start asking to go home?"

As Mike began chattering, neither of his parents could remain indifferent to his enthusiasm. Jumping from one item of interest to another, he recounted details of trips to the canteen, the farm, the water tanks, and the small circus that had recently visited the Children's Unit for a special performance. As he rattled on, he looked eagerly from one to the other and it was obvious that, as far as Mike was concerned, the lonely years were over and he was ready at last to become a member of the family. There was nothing to indicate that he held anything against them.

Mike's parents were quiet, listening attentively, although they didn't have much choice—it would have been impossible for anyone to get a word in edgewise. Through it all, his mother watched him intently.

Finally I interrupted him.

"Mike evidently wants to share with you everything that's happened to him. Would you like to go for a walk around the grounds? Perhaps Mike could show you the cactus-rock garden he built with his friend Danny."

The Harrises readily agreed.

"Mike, after you've shown your folks around, will you bring them back here, please?"

"Okay. We go now, we *gooooooo!!*" Mike jumped up and stuck out his hand. "Heah, Mommy, take my hahnd. You too, Dahdee," and he thrust his hand into his father's.

As the three of them left, Mike eagerly pulling his parents along, both Mr. and Mrs. Harris looked back at me. They were smiling—joyful, but still disbelieving. A half-hour later they returned, looking rather harried, but happy.

"Mike, you say good-bye to your folks now. It's almost time for your meds, so you'd better skedaddle back up to the cottage. Why don't you give them a hug good-bye like you give me, Mike?"

He nodded vigorously and gave each of his parents a big hug, wrapping his arms around them and squeezing.

"G'bye Mommy, g'bye, Dahdee—when cahn I go for hoome bisit?"

"Let me talk with your parents now, Mike. We'll talk about a home visit later."

Mike's face squinched up in mild disapproval. Reluctantly, he backed out of the room and, after a few moments for a last look, he disappeared down the hall.

When he'd gone, I said, "It looks like Mike gave you quite a tour."

Both of them seemed overwhelmed, almost to the point of stupefaction. We sat in silence awhile, Mrs. Harris seemingly replaying the events in her mind because every now and then she shook her head. Finally Mr. Harris, obviously moved, cleared his throat.

"Well, Mikey *is* very different. Beats me how you did it!"

Over the next half-hour, I briefly outlined what had happened during the last two years. When I mentioned the "hikers' rule" of helping each other, Mr. Harris nodded.

"So that's why Mike wanted me to climb up the bluff with him. We started to, but before long I was beginning to puff pretty good and I stopped. Mike had already gotten a ways up, but when he saw I'd stopped, he came back down the hill and said somethin' about that—hikers working together. Then he took my hand and started pulling me!"

"That's what a super guy he is, Mr. Harris. And that's why I'd like to see the two of you get more involved with him now. Of course, it's really up to you, but we'll be glad to work with you and help out in any way we can. Initially, maybe you could come up to see him a few more times, and then if that goes all right, eventually we could try a home visit." They seemed uncertain about that, so I added, "Just think about it, talk it over together, and let me know what you decide."

Mr. Harris looked at his wife and an understanding seemed to pass unspoken between them.

"Well, it'd be okay with us," he said. "If you doctors think he's ready. Then maybe we'll see about that home visit he wants so bad."

"Fine, we'll set up some times for you to come out, then."

I happened to be at Cottage 4 a week later when Mike came bounding in the door, towing his parents. He announced to all within earshot, "My Dahdee ahn' Mommy brought me *cahndee!*" He was holding a rumpled paper bag and his grin was laced with caramel and nuts. Quickly Mike opened the bag and offered me a piece. Then he spotted Jody.

"You want some, Jo-dee?"

She nodded, smiling, and with great ceremony Mike placed a selected piece in her palm. Then he clutched the sack to himself as if it were gold.

Chuck, coffee cup in hand, came down the corridor.

"I got cahndee, Chahk—you want some?" Mike opened the sack again and peered in with Chuck. "Those ah good—" he said.

"Okay, I'll try that one, Mike. Thank you."

"You welcahm, Chahk." Mike turned and grinned at me. That was something he had learned to say a month ago, and he rarely missed an opportunity to use it.

During this time, Mike's parents had stood to the side watching the scene unfold.

"I think your folks probably need to get back now, Mike," I said. "Are you going to hug them good-bye?"

"Okay." Mike swooped over to where they were waiting and, as each bent down, he curled his arms around them and embraced them. Then he stepped back.

"Didn't you forget to say something, Mike?" I asked.

He beamed. "Tonk you for comin' Mommy ahn' Dahdee. When cahn you come again?"

That was nearly too much for the Harrises; their eyes filled with tears as they said their good-byes. I left the cottage with them. As we reached the walk by the side of the building, a rattling from the dayroom window caused us to turn. There was Mike, his grinning face pressed up against the glass, waving vigorously. We all waved back.

Near the parking lot, Mr. and Mrs. Harris both stopped. They stood there, uncomfortably shifting their feet, apparently with something on their minds. Finally, Mr. Harris found his voice. Taking his wife's hand in his, he said, "Dr. McGarry, we both want to thank you, you've done a lot for Mike. He's really so much better. Long ago we'd given up hope that he could ever be like he is now . . . "

Then it was my turn to feel awkward. I have never been very adept at accepting compliments, so I mumbled something to the effect that it was actually the team, the staff, who deserved the credit. And, of course, Mike. Embarrassed, we stood together, unable to put what we wanted to say into words. But then, there wasn't really any need to do so.

The hospital visits continued to go well and a month later Mike went on his first weekend trip home. It included a long car ride, a trip to the zoo, and a Walt Disney movie. Although Mike's parents admitted he was a handful, his energy leaving them exhausted, when they returned to the hospital on Sunday afternoon they were eager to make arrangements for another home visit. Mike couldn't have been happier.

CHAPTER EIGHTEEN

Scott and I were just polishing off our morning coffee when his telephone rang. It was long-distance, so I went back to my own office. Twenty minutes later, he appeared in the doorway.

"That was a friend of mine in Wisconsin. Teaches there. Wanted to know if I knew of anyone who'd like a good job opportunity—it combines teaching with clinical practice with kids."

I shrugged. "Can't think of anyone offhand."

"Actually, I thought perhaps you might be interested."

"Me? Hey, what is this? You trying to get rid of me?"

Scott smiled and shook his head. "Just thought I'd mention it. There're some fine clinicians in the group, good psychotherapists. They could teach you a bit, build up your professional credentials. It'd be a definite step up. But if you'd rather not . . . "

"Well, if I were looking for something else—which I'm not—Wisconsin wouldn't be my first choice, anyway. It's the boonies, isn't it?"

"Not really. I think you'd like the Midwest. It's a nice

place to live; the people are the salt of the earth." He grinned. "I grew up there."

"But Scott, I'm happy here. And besides, there's Mike to consider."

"I know, it'd be rough for him at first."

"To say the least."

"But I think Mike is strong enough now to handle separation. We could work out a way to transfer him to someone else. In fact, this would be as good a time as any to do it. You've gotten awfully attached to each other, and actually it might be better for him in the long run if he had a different therapist before long. It would broaden his base, help him to adapt better to change. He's very dependent on you. And then, of course, some new experiences would be good for you, too."

"Well, I don't know—"

"Think about it, anyway. I wouldn't let your concern for Mike stand in the way. I certainly don't want to lose you, Pat, but this sounds like a strong group, a good program. Might be worth checking it out."

"Okay, Scott, I guess I can at least do that."

The next day I called Wisconsin and had a long conversation with the chief psychologist. By the time I hung up, I had agreed to go for an interview. No question about it—this was an impressive opportunity.

My main worry was the risk to Mike. Despite Scott's words, I was afraid that Mike might interpret my leaving as abandonment, as one more person—indeed, the very one who had promised never to do so—"looking the other way." At the same time, though, I had to admit that Scott was right. As attached as Mike was to me, he was also reaching out to the staff and the kids around him as well as forming a new, positive relationship with his parents.

Perhaps it *was* time for me to move out of the center of his life and leave the space open for him to develop. If I did leave, however, I would have to be certain that Mike understood my reasons and plans, so that he wouldn't take my departure as rejection.

Two weeks later I flew to Wisconsin. The countryside was a picture right out of my fifth-grade geography book— red barns, black-and-white cows, crisp rivers, and placid lakes surrounded by lush greenery. They offered me the position, but I begged off letting them know immediately. I just wasn't sure, so I returned home to mull it over. Finally, at about the last moment, I decided to accept the appointment. Slightly over two months remained for me to prepare Mike.

As I thought about possible therapists, my mind kept returning to Debbie. She would be ideal. Not only was she a warm and caring person, she was also an avid backpacker. All of the kids thought the world of her. Even Mike had remarked about the fun they had had on a recent outing to the beach. When I mentioned the idea to Debbie, she agreed immediately, saying she liked Mike and would be happy to take over with him.

"After all," she grinned, "you've already done the hard part! And frankly, the chance to go hiking really appeals to me."

Scott supported the arrangement, pointing out the potential benefits for Mike of having first a male therapist and then a female therapist as role models. But everything depended on how Mike reacted to Debbie, whether he'd respond to her, accept her. The next time I went to Mike's cottage to pick him up, Debbie went with me.

He seemed surprised but pleased when I told him that Debbie wanted to go on a hike with us, and he readily agreed with my suggestion that he show her some of the more interesting places we'd discovered on Dogface. More than once I caught him looking at her out of the corner of his eye. Lithe and deeply tanned, with a quick engaging smile and long auburn hair worn free, Debbie was extremely attractive. And Mike had obviously noticed. He was, I thought to myself, getting to that age. I was sure that he had never seen a woman quite like her. The ones he was used to—primarily nurses—all dressed in white uniforms. And Cecile was an older woman who had grandchildren Mike's age.

Initially, he was very bashful around Debbie, but she adroitly put him at ease. Changing into her "grubbies"— faded Levi's and a T-shirt—and anchoring her hair with a blue paisley scarf before setting out, Debbie slid easily into the routine. Over the next several weeks the three of us thoroughly scoured Dogface, hiking up to the summit and returning to the canteen for refreshments. Mike took great pride in showing Debbie around the water filtration plant, the farm, the water tanks, even teaching her the names of the trees. He seemed more than happy to include her in all our activities, although he frequently walked next to me, holding my hand and positioning me between him and Debbie.

One day an incident occurred that really made me smile. We were coming back down the trail from the crest when Mike, clambering among the boulders, found himself overextended and stranded on a ledge leading to a drop of several feet. He needed assistance.

"Some-bahdy help me . . . "

Debbie, who was closer, stepped over near him.

"C'mon, Mike, you can climb down from there by yourself. It's not that high."

Mike stared down at her for several seconds, then drew himself up to his full, gangly height. Waggling his finger at Debbie, he said reproachfully, "Hikas hahfta work togethuh!"

Debbie looked at me, chagrin written clearly across her face. Then she began climbing up to where Mike was.

"You're absolutely right, Mike—hikers *do* have to work together. C'mon now, give me your hand."

He accepted readily and they scrambled down the short wall. Later, after we had returned to the administrative cottage, Debbie mentioned Mike's rebuke.

"He made me feel that high!" she winced.

"That's okay," I countered. "He's done that to me lots of times. Anyway, it was just a little testing for you. I suspect he knows he's breaking you in as his new therapist."

I figured Mike would surmise that I was leaving. After all, he was a very sensitive kid who didn't miss much—those little antennae were always out there waving around.

But with only five weeks left before my departure, it was time for me to have a talk with him. I had rehearsed in my mind a hundred different ways of telling him I was leaving, but none seemed any easier than the others. I was dreading the whole thing. The most harrowing fantasy was that perhaps he would immediately and irretrievably melt back into his shell. There was just no way of predicting how Mike would react. The longer I put off telling him, the more anxious I got about it. I couldn't delay any longer.

The following day Mike, Debbie, and I went for a short hike and then stopped at the canteen for ice cream cones. I had forewarned Debbie, so she excused herself early to return to the unit while Mike and I wandered down to some nearby trees along the dry creek bed to finish our ice cream. Settling comfortably under an old willow tree, I summoned up my courage as Mike scrambled in pursuit of a sunning lizard. After watching him for a few minutes, I said,

"Mike, I want to talk with you."

He paused and glanced quickly over at me. Something in my voice arrested him and, forgetting the lizard, he scuffed over to me, a serious look on his face.

"Sit down here beside me for a minute, okay?" I patted the nearby grass.

Mike flopped down cross-legged, leaning his back against the trunk of the willow.

"Mike, we've been good friends, hiking buddies, for quite a while now, haven't we?"

He nodded soberly.

"And you know that during this last year I finally became a doctor—a doctor who is going to work with girls and boys like you who have problems and have to come to a hospital like this one."

Mike nodded again.

"Now Mike, I've been offered a position—a job—at a place far away from here. I can work with some people there who can teach me much more than I know now about helping kids. But to do that, Mike, I have to go away. I've thought about it a lot—believe me, it's been one of the hardest decisions I've ever had to make. But I feel I have to do it. Mike, I'm going to be going away . . . "

Up to this point Mike had been watching me, his eyes darting around nervously. Now as he finally heard me acknowledge my leaving, a look of desolation spread over his face. Almost immediately his eyes shifted away and gazed out at some point above my shoulder. I recognized the same expression I'd seen that afternoon on Dogface so long ago just before he made the decision to reach out and give me his hand, to trust me.

"Mike—" I began falteringly, "I do love you and we've been the best of buddies. But sometimes people have to go on to new things, different things. And sometimes that means they have to leave someone who's very special. It hurts a lot to have to separate, and I feel really bad because I know this is hurting you. Believe me, that's the last thing in the world I'd want to do to my hiking buddy. Can you understand that, Mike?"

His eyes shifted back to me, his face flushed and contorted as he tried not to cry.

"Mike—" I put my arms out, and with a little whimper his muffled sobs were buried in my shoulder.

And I cried right along with him, intensely sorry to have caused this pain, wondering whether I had indeed made the right decision. But at the same time, I was relieved that at last he knew.

After a few minutes we both sat quietly, my arm still around his shoulders. Finally he gazed up at me, his red-rimmed eyes and dirt-streaked face set, but his voice faltering a bit.

"Hike Dogfahs a liddo ways, Paht?"

Giving him another big hug, I said to him, "Sure, Mike. You know, you're one spunky kid!"

During the next few weeks, I took some time at each of our meetings to talk with him about my leaving. Debbie would always take off early while Mike and I walked slowly back to the cottage together. Other times we sat and talked in his room, surrounded by his pictures of our hikes and the other places we'd visited and things we'd done together. It was important that Mike fully understand that I was really going away. But it was even more vital that we talk about our relationship and how he felt about my departure. At first the discussions took a fairly predictable direction.

"But why do you hahfta go, Paht—don't you like it

heah?" . . . "Why cahn't you learn to be a betta docta heah?" . . . "If you leaf, you cahn't hike up Dogfahs."

I tried to help Mike reach a balance, to understand the feelings he had toward me, and to recognize that there would always be an element of risk involved whenever he got close to someone. And Mike continued to astound me with his ability to grasp these concepts.

One day I told him, "You know, Mike, even grown-ups have trouble with all this—loving someone, caring deeply, and taking the risk of opening themselves up to others. That's scary because it's always possible that the other person may not return their affection or might someday leave them. It's a really tough thing to deal with."

Mike met my eyes with an intensely perceptive look. "You mean like when Debbie was—" he searched for the word, trying to grapple with something he didn't understand, "—when Debbie was dee-borse ahn' she was unhahppy . . . "

I just stared at him. Debbie's recent divorce was more or less a secret. In fact, most of the staff hadn't known what was going on.

"How did you find out about that, Mike? Do you know what it means when you say she was divorced?"

He shrugged. "Nuh. But I saw Debbie—ahn' she was crying. I nevuh saw a grown-up cry. She few bahd?"

I shook my head, amazed by his forthright logic.

"Well yes, she felt bad. When two people have been married and they're not happy together, sometimes it's better for them to separate and not live together anymore. That's what divorce is, and it can be very painful. But there are also other kinds of separation that are difficult to adjust to. Like when someone dies and everyone feels sad inside and misses him. Or when people have to stay in the hospital for a long time like you have and they're away from their families. They miss their folks very much. I think your mother and father have missed you a lot all these years. It's been very hard for them."

Mike looked away for several moments, struggling to reconcile this jumble of ideas. At last he said, "Ah Mommy ahn' Dahdee go-ing to come ahn' get me ahn' take me hoome?"

"Well, Mike, I just don't know about that. Certainly they will take you on more home visits so all of you can spend some time together. Perhaps eventually it would be for good. Would you like to go and live at home?"

"Yes, I would—vewy much!"

"Well, we'll have to see about that. In the meantime, you just keep doing as great as you have been and maybe things will work out that way. Keep on drawing all those nice pictures, going to the playroom with Debbie, and learning in school. But especially, Mike, stay the super person you are, always doing things for other people and letting them do things for you—just being nice to them the way you are. You know, everyone really likes you a lot. Did you know that?"

He shook his head, squirming and blushing with embarrassment.

"Well, they do—very much. Because you're such a nice person. And you like them, too, don't you? That's what it's all about, isn't it?"

He nodded, still self-conscious and bashful.

There were many talks like this and gradually Mike seemed to begin to accept my leaving. One day in school, he showed Cecile a picture that he had just drawn, saying, "This is my friend, Paht, and this is me—Mik'l. Paht is go-ing fah away, ahn' he won't be able to hike with Mik'l on Dogfahs anymore . . . or go to cahn-teen . . ."

An occasional report filtered back to me from the cottage, too. For instance, one evening a television program contained a tearful leave-taking, and as Mike made the connection an aide overheard him say softly to himself, "Paht is leaf-ing, too. Paht is my friend . . . "

One warm afternoon in late summer, over a month after we'd first included Debbie in our activities, she joined us again for a hike. We had climbed to Mike's favorite spot on Dogface and now we were relaxing on the crest, idly talking and joking, when Mike abruptly turned to Debbie with the candor only a child can muster.

"Once I saw you cry. On the baseball field."

Debbie looked surprised, then nodded.

"I saw you crying when you got dee-borse. You fewt bahd . . . it hurt you . . . " The statements were tentative, searching.

"Yes, it did, Mike. Whenever something like that happens, it hurts—a lot. You and Pat are feeling bad now because Pat's moving so far away. That hurts inside, too, because you're going to miss each other very much. Isn't that right?"

Mike nodded. He seemed lost in thought and Debbie and I exchanged concerned looks.

After a while we started back down the hill, in no particular hurry and somewhat reluctant to return to the hospital. Mike seemed oddly subdued; that wasn't like him and I wondered what was up. By the time we reached the quad, we were walking three abreast, Mike in the middle, and he was holding my hand.

Suddenly, with incredible enthusiasm, he exclaimed, "*I* know! *Debbie* cahn be my new friend!!"

Without breaking stride, he reached out and clutched Debbie's hand, the ultimate gesture of acceptance. Over his head, Debbie and I smiled at each other.

"That sounds like a great idea, Mike," I said. Then all three of us stopped, looked from one to the other, and burst out laughing.

Debbie and I wondered aloud why *we* hadn't thought of such a fine idea, but Mike was impervious to such conjecture—he had found a solution to the problem all by himself. The rest of the way back to the cottage, Mike skipped along between us, holding both our hands.

As for me, I felt as though the entire weight of Dogface had suddenly been lifted from my shoulders. The reaction was, of course, exactly what we'd planned and hoped for, but it was significant that Mike had initiated the final choice on his own. The following days substantiated his decision as reports accumulated from those in contact with Mike that he was telling everyone who would listen, "Debbie is go-ing to be my new friend ahn' hike with me on Dogfahs ahn' take me to th' playroom. Debbie is my new friend . . . "

During our final meetings, I tended to become less involved as the relationship between Mike and Debbie began to flourish. And Mike slowly pulled back from me as he spent more time with his "new friend."

I was ready to leave. I had said my farewells to the staff at a going-away party on the unit and then Scott and I walked down to his office. I eased into the familiar red leather chair, stretching my legs out. "I've spent a few hours in this baby," I said.

Scott selected a pipe and proceeded with the established ritual. By mutual accord, we had grown accustomed to using that time to collect ourselves, and our thoughts. After those moments of preparation, Scott peered at me through the tangy smoke.

"How's the packing going?"

"Slowly."

"Still not too sure that you made the right decision?"

"No, I guess not, Scott."

We sat in silence.

"Mike?"

"He's doing fine so far. It's other things, too, I guess."

"Like . . . "

"Well, I don't know exactly where to begin. You know, Scott, it's like my life before coming here just flowed along and I never fully appreciated how lucky I am. I took so much for granted—my parents always being there, being supportive, caring, giving me the freedom to do whatever seemed right at the moment. Now I'm so much more aware of people and relationships. Of not taking anyone for granted. I look at my parents—they're getting older now, worried because I'll be living so far away—and I'm finally getting around to appreciating them, saying thank you. And, of course, they know what brought it all home . . . literally. A goofy little kid who buzzed around this place and about drove me up the wall. It's been shock therapy for me."

Scott nodded, watching me closely.

"And my teachers—you, Warfield, and others—all of you set expectations for me. High ones. But what you really did was believe in me, in my ability to figure things out, excel at whatever I chose to do. And that helped me to believe in myself. Parts of me have been reached that I didn't know I had, and I'll never be the same . . . "

Scott was examining his pipe in minute detail. Then he said, "It really works both ways, Pat. It's been rewarding for me, too, seeing you grow and mature. And that's where a major part of professional and personal satisfaction comes from—not only from helping the troubled, but also from enhancing the skills of someone like you who is entering the field. This power of understanding and caring, and certainly love, is of such significance I'm sure you'll carry it with you the rest of your life.

"And now you're off for more challenges. I'm sure there'll be many more professional successes like the one you've had with Mike. But I can tell you this—no matter how many people you help over the years as a psychotherapist, there'll always be one who will be very special, one who will always come to mind when you reflect upon your work. Because Mike was the very first—and a pretty tough customer—but you did it."

At last I went searching for Mike to say my final goodbye to him. We sat in his room under the myriad of Dogface pictures, neither of us wanting to resurrect the gearing-down of feelings and involvement that was occurring inside both of us. I made my farewell brief.

"Mike, you've been a very good buddy, and I want you to know how much I appreciate your willingness to share so much with me. We've both come a long way together . . . "

Mike sat on his bed, looking down at the floor. Slowly he reached behind him and handed me a rolled-up paper tied with a green ribbon. Shyly, he said, "This is fur you, Paht. From me—"

I slipped off the ribbon and unrolled the paper. "Thank you, Mike." My voice caught and "Mike" came out as a throaty whisper. I gave him a quick hug and moved to the door. "We'll see each other again, Mike. I promise . . ."

He nodded, glancing briefly at me, then lowered his head again and blinked back the tears. As I left he remained there, poised quietly on the edge of his bed, and once again I thought how special he was. I was sure he'd make it. Really, he'd made it already.

Out in the parking lot I gazed for a few moments at the silhouette of Dogface, set ablaze by the red-orange rays of the late afternoon sun. Then I picked up the picture Mike had given me and looked at it for a long time. It was a "cooperative" drawing we had done several months ago— started by me, finished by Mike.

I set it down on the seat beside me, shaking my head. Something momentous had happened to me here—something, as Scott had said, that would be a part of me for the rest of my life.

A movement caught my eye and I turned to see three small children making their way back from the riverbed. From this distance they looked like any other children, not the exceptional ones they were. I remembered that that had been my impression on my very first day at the hospital. The day I had spotted that little urchin scurrying along the wall.

What extraordinary experiences, and extraordinary people, I had met here. With a heavy sigh, I turned the key in the ignition and then retraced the winding road that would take me away from the hospital and halfway across the country.

CHAPTER NINETEEN

SINCE I LEFT CALIFORNIA, DEBBIE HAS HELPED MIKE WRITE and draw picture-letters to me that relate his continuing activities. It's difficult to know just how complete his recovery will be. There is little doubt that the early and severe onset of schizophrenia arrested his development. Along with that handicap, the dimension of living in a hospital for many years can produce a large degree of dependence. It may be that Mike will always need a certain measure of professional help. But he's a fighter and, with time and treatment, he may just be able to put it all behind him.

For myself, I can now better understand why what happened between Mike and me was significant—not only for him, but for me as well. Each of us was ready for the other. My enthusiasm was genuine, if a bit misdirected at times. I had a lot of energy, fueled by idealism, and a good hunch that I could reach that forlorn kid. As a psychotherapist, I've learned to value that kind of intuition.

I also believe that very early in the game, Mike sensed all that in me. The layers of hurt and rejection ran deep, but underneath was a child—a tentative little creature who yearned only to be understood, cared for, loved. But until someone came along who could find a way to gain his trust, Mike had waited, like a dormant plant, for the warming winds of spring.

A NOTE ABOUT THE AUTHOR

A NATIVE CALIFORNIAN OF MAVERICK IRISH extraction, Robert Lane has long been fascinated by human behavior. After receiving his Ph.D. from the University of Wisconsin, Madison, he worked as a clinical psychologist in various mental institutions and treatment centers in the Midwest. Dr. Lane is now on the faculty of the University of Wisconsin, Oshkosh. He and his wife Mary live on the shore of the legendary Lake Butte des Morts.

A NOTE ON THE TYPE

THE TEXT OF THIS BOOK IS SET IN 11 POINT COMPUGRAPHIC Sabon, designed in 1964 by Jan Tschichold to accommodate a seventeenth century typeface to a modern typographic technology. The Sabon typeface has a noble lineage: it is a descendant of one of the greatest designs in typographic history—Garamond. Originally crafted in France by Claude Garamont in early 1500, Garamond is considered the first "true" printing letter face—that is, it didn't have a handcut look. In 1615 Garamond was recut by Jean Jannon and since then a whole family of typefaces, such as Sabon, have evolved. The elegance and grace of the typestyle have assured it a distinctive position in the history of printing.

The chapter and running heads are in Korinna, a typestyle created in 1904 and subsequently refined into a most versatile and unique design.

A goodly number of people in Wisconsin's Fox River Valley contributed to the production of this book. Mary Lane was responsible for the copy editing and book design. Tom and Carole Stinski of The Composing Room in Kimberly set the text film. Beulah Seager corrected the proofs. Paul Donhauser and John Iwata contributed cover design suggestions. Cover film was prepared by Northwestern Colorgraphics. The volume was printed and bound by the George Banta Company of Menasha.